In 1920 an English poet, David G[oodchild, arrived at] an institution in Derbyshire run [by an American psychiatrist, Clive] Penn, and his wife Mary. It was intended that David should be a houseguest initially, and thereafter a patient, because his mind had been damaged by the war. Dr Penn liked the idea of treating a poet: perhaps they could unravel the psychopathology of poetry. And Mary liked the idea even more: she had always wanted a poet. She invited David into her sitting room while Dr Penn visited his other patients.

Mary grew fond of David.

It was a time when psychiatry was just emerging and for Mary to have married a psychiatrist was considered 'modern'; to have married an American psychiatrist even more so. Yet it was Mary who tried to prevent her husband from integrating his patients into the village – who warned him that what was normal on the Western Front, or what was fashionable in Vienna and London did not necessarily hold in Derbyshire. Just because the doctor had not heard the words 'cowardice' or 'lunatic' did not mean they weren't lurking behind a British reserve he hadn't quite fathomed. Mary's words were prophetic. Through his deeply affecting narrative, Richard Burns leads us into a compelling investigation of the personal consequences of war – when the fear and danger an individual has lived through leave no alternative but retreat into a form of mental disorder. He sympathetically and memorably portrays Goodchild as a poet, Georgian at heart, who cannot face modernity and, even less, the stigma of failure in the ghastly arena of combat he never wished to enter.

BY THE SAME AUTHOR
THE PANDA HUNT
KHALINDAINE
TROUBADOUR
WHY DIAMOND HAD TO DIE
FOND AND FOOLISH LOVERS

A Dance for the Moon
Richard Burns

BLOOMSBURY

First published in Great Britain 1986

Copyright © 1986 by Richard Burns

This paperback edition published 1991

The moral right of the author has been asserted

Bloomsbury Publishing Ltd, 2 Soho Square, London W1V 5DE

A CIP catalogue record for this book
is available from the British Library

ISBN 0 7475 0929 8

All rights reserved: no part of this publication
may be reproduced, stored in a retrieval system, or transmitted
in any form or by any means, electronic, mechanical, photocopying
or otherwise, without the prior written permission of the publisher.

Printed in Great Britain by
Cox and Wyman Limited, Reading, Berkshire.

To Sharon

THE HOUSE STOOD well back from the road, and thus a sensation was avoided, for when David, stark naked, climbed on to the roof, only the servants could see. Mrs Goodchild was informed at once, of course, and ran out to the lawn. She looked up at the Regency roof with its low ornamental balustrade.

'Mother!' David called when he saw her. He was sitting astride the roof with his back to one of the chimneys. 'Isn't it a splendid day?' He was twenty-four years old. He had not been well since the war.

He stood up. His buttocks were scored with the impression of the pantiles. 'I can see such a very long way.' Leaning his weight backwards to help him balance he walked down the roof to the balustrade. His penis was a scrawny white cuckoo in a nest of black hair, and one of the maids giggled.

He stood at the guttering which marked the eaves. 'The Grand Old Duke of York,' he recited, turning to climb, 'He had ten thousand men. He marched them up to the top of the hill . . . ' David paused, establishing himself in a dramatic pose on the hip of the roof, and then turned and scampered down: 'And he marched them down again.'

The tempo of climb and descent increased. 'And when they were up they were up. And when they were down they were down. And when they were only half-way up, they . . . ' A dislodged tile slid down the roof, through the balustrade, and smashed into clean orange shards on the terrace three floors below. At the noise David threw himself, whimpering and clinging, flat against the roof. He was still crying when Burton, the gardener, helped him down.

CHAPTER ONE

A TUSSLE OF steam chuffed the sky: the journey was under way. The station clock said ten to ten; knowing schoolboys wrote down numbers; hands and relatives disappeared. The scene broadened about the train: they passed narrow streets and allotments, and the allotments were portents of fields; ahead were meadows and brooks, while behind them Gloucester spread like a fan, and the single tower of the cathedral was guarded by suburban gas holders.

Two engines pulled the train. The first was an old Johnson 'spinner', No 677; behind was a three-cylinder compound, a 4-4-0. Both engines were painted Midland Railway's crimson lake, lined in yellow and black, and were clouding the air with white plumes.

Through Churchdown and on into Cheltenham they went, with the Cotswold hills to their right. Summer had turned into autumn: the trees were filament and filigree beneath a stained grey sky. There was a hint of snow beneath the walls at the top of the hills. The train pulled out of Cheltenham, and through Banbury line junction, Honeybury line junction, Lansdown and Cleeve and Ashchurch. They were into Worcestershire now: Bredon, Eckington, Defford, Wadborough. North of Abbotswood junction they passed under the Great Western line, their smoking steam, like a wake, converging with that of a heavy green engine that tugged at a line of brown trucks.

Then they were through the goods yards of Spetchley and Droitwich Road, and at the foot of the Lickey Incline, where they waited: the great Lickey banking engine, Big Bertha, passed alongside and then pushed from behind, shoving them up the long gradient.

The train heaved and strained itself north, up a line cut into a hill; David sat back in his comfortable seat and lit a cigarette. They reached the summit; David blew the smoke out. He watched the patterns his smoke made: a coil and a cone and then nothing. His mother sat opposite, facing him and the rear of the train. He smiled at her but she was looking outside.

The snow was clotting with buildings, and then the buildings came in at the line. They came with a rush, threatening the windows, and then they scaled upwards as the train ran into a cutting. The cutting surged, urged the train noises at them, and David hummed in the loudness.

He looked out. Beyond the cutting the buildings fell away to below the level of the track, and the snow had almost gone. Glistening black roofs angled up to the embankment, supervised by stiff and disapproving spires. The train passed the back of soiled houses, where milk-cans were left by the doors, and crossed black and white streets that were flicked with hurrying figures. Station name-plates were seen, fixed, and whisked away – Bournville, Selly Oak, Somerset Road – until, like a creature that lives in its own filth, they entered unlit tunnels that stank of smoke, and emerged into Birmingham New Street.

The canopy arched wide above them; the train shuffled to a halt. People climbed off and people climbed on. Mrs Goodchild looked across at David. Dear David, so handsome, so gifted. She recalled with pride Eddie Marsh's remark – 'David is the best English lyric poet I've read since Rupert Brooke' – and the poem that had inspired that verdict.

> A quiver of air, a voice
> Is also a quiver of arrows,
>
> While truth is the air in a vase,
> Inseparable, undisturbed.

The gentle light of an autumn noon, with comically English reserve, warmed his face and the wave of his fair hair. It was a good face, with firm cheekbones and a fine, narrow nose; the blond moustache, to his mother's indulgent eye, made him look younger, and was vaguely absurd.

If only, she thought, he could get his health back.

The train pulled out from beneath the high and pigeon-roosted canopy. Saltley, Kingbury, Wilnecote, Tamworth: she stopped looking at the stations and let the sound of the train, the flashed rhythm of the telegraph poles past the window, soothe her half-way to sleep.

She dozed and tried to picture their destination: Dr Penn, Winfell, Grindlow, near Sheffield. Sheffield was black in her imagination, and was crushed and smutted with smoke; she had stayed as a girl at a place called Winfell, but that had been in the Lake District. She made hills and lakes in her mind, rilled with rivers of molten steel, and placed a grey sanatorium there, beneath a fat grey moon. The sanatorium was very like her home. She jerked and tried again.

She tried to imagine the doctor. She had not yet met him, but had learnt something of him from nosy friends and helpful acquaintances – Lady Lougham knew his mother-in-law, apparently; Mrs Denville-Thompson had a nephew who had a friend at Winfell. From a mosaic of second-hand impressions she had formed an impression of her own. He was young – under forty, she knew – and was an American, but he had served in the British army in the war. Mrs Goodchild rather approved of that: it appeared he had been studying at Cambridge when the war was declared. He had won the MC. She saw him straight-backed and casually dressed, as befitted an ex-officer who was also American, with a trim and medical beard that turned grey as it mixed with his hair.

Images met and mingled. Dr Penn stood on the moonlit sward, looking out at the black waters of the lake. The house was bigger than before. Its casements were all shuttered. Then the images attained motion and turned into a dream.

The train rattled on. The wheels travelled the points and tackled the miles; the engine ousted white steam. David saw his mother's head weighing heavy on her chest. They passed a town he could not name and crossed a turgid river. They ran alongside a road, overtaking a horse and two-wheeler. Children waved from the trap and David smiled back at them.

They reached another large town. Its skyline was broken by curious towers that were like bent tunnels trying to scratch the low clouds. The train slowed. They passed a signal box, and he could read 'Burton-on-Trent' in cream-on-crimson nailed to its front. They reached the station and stopped.

Mrs Goodchild raised her head and blinked. For a moment she found she had forgotten where she was; then she remembered. The station clock said quarter past twelve: they were half-way there. David was looking out of the window. Along the platform dark-coated people strode by, or lugged great suitcases that were like recalcitrant pets. Doors slammed the length of the train. A whistle blew. And David, hearing these sounds, shivered and turned pale.

The mud has soaked identity away; I cannot even tell if these are British dead. I look round from the shelter of this shallow captured trench, but there is nothing to see. The battle is hidden behind smoke.

The smoke has many textures: sometimes wispy, like

the cigarette smoke of the rifles, slightly blue in the once-blue day. The cigar-mortar clogs more effectively, and gathers in the folds of dead men's uniforms. The piping shells whistle all around, and their heavy smoke is made mustard with dust. My ears smart desperately. I do not like the smoke.

I cannot see through the smoke that is in my eyes and beyond my eyes, so my other senses must work for me. I smell the sharpness of explosives and the bluntness of sweat; my body quakes with the percussion of the shells; in my mouth fear tastes of warm decay; in my ears the whole war sounds. I hear the wail and spread of the shells as they smash and scatter the soil. Sometimes one lands in the black river beside us, sending up a roar and a spray of fine sounds. I hear machine-guns splinter the air. I hear the quick smart clap of the rifles. And behind it all, I hear the silence of the dead.

Mrs Goodchild turned from the window, and was shocked by what she saw. His eyes were tightly closed and his mouth tugged by harsh shallow breaths. She stretched her hand across at him but he did not respond. She had to fumble one of his hands free before she could hold it and reassure him.

'There, there,' she said, made vulnerable by the inadequacy of her own response. 'There, there. It's all right. There, there.'

At length he opened his eyes to her. He regarded her blankly, as if he too were coming back from a dream. Then she registered.

'Sometimes I forget that it is now,' he said. He smiled weakly to reassure her, and the smile squeezed two tears from his eyes.

'Gently, gently,' she murmured. 'Everything will be all right. You'll see. Everything'll be fine.'

He softly disengaged his hand from hers and sat back in his seat. Outside, the fecund railway lines were multiplying; they entered Derby. They passed long grey sheds, lit by the clerestory. Coupled coaches lined their route. They passed a string of Pullman carriages, brown and cream, named 'Jane' and 'Anne' and 'Lizobel'.

'I'm all right now,' said David. 'It wasn't a bad one.'

He lit himself a cigarette, and pointed things out to his mother. Crimson engines plying their steam; coaches waiting in leisurely lengths; dumpy grey trucks clumped together. Three boys in red blazers looked down from a bridge, noting the particulars of each engine, and as their train trundled slowly through the yards, David waved.

Mrs Goodchild found herself wishing she were not sitting opposite David. She could think of nowhere to look except at him, and she did not want to show her concern. He certainly appears better, she thought, but she knew it was a fragile show. She looked away from him.

'It's raining,' she said in surprise.

She studied the clouds instead of her son. The quality of clouds is most strange, she discovered: they are hard and yet soft, pewter that is flaccid, and they do not diminish when they shed their rain. The train stood in the station; drops of water speckled the window. Each spot was a crescent of black and a white highlight. Then the train pulled away, and the spots became streaks without form.

The weather was worse at Winfell: the last dregs of daylight fell as sleet, illuminated by the light through the windows and slashing the darkening sky. The wind made spasms of gritty noise on the panes; Mary, in her armchair, read a poem. It was by David.

> When lying in a shell-hole by the wire
> I often thought of my return.
> You'd be standing on the dappled lawn,
> Your face would wear an immaculate smile,
> And I'd be limping. The swift spring smell

Of mayflower frothing in the lane
Would catch our kiss and quite atone
For the rancid stench on the breath of war
And the easy death that is life on the line.

Well, the war is over, and at last
I've returned; it's autumn of course,
The trees are either sleeping or dead,
But that isn't the only difference:
Your forced smile and your careful deference
As you discover just what the war did
And learn what's meant by a 'shell-shock case'
Show a laboured love that will soon be lost.
I'm sorry, dearest. I should have died.

She had found the poem in an edition of *Georgian Poetry*, soon after she had first heard David was to come to Winfell. Now she read it every night.

The doctor looked into the sitting-room and saw his wife curled up in her chair, her legs beneath her, with the yellow-backed book resting on her arm.

'Hello, darling,' he called. 'I'm back.'

She did not look up. 'Hello dear,' she said. 'Did you get wet?' There was firelight along her downy skin and in her hair: the doctor thought her beautiful.

'Very,' he replied.

He crossed the narrow corridor and went into their bedroom. Their living accommodation at Winfell was cramped, for even though the patients no longer lived in the house, much of it was given over to offices and stores. He had left his wet overcoat downstairs, and his galoshes, but his trousers and socks were soaked through at his ankles. He took his jacket and trousers off quickly, and went to the wardrobe in search of a change of clothes.

There was a mirror on the inside of the wardrobe door. He saw himself there: a healthy looking man of almost middle age; his white legs were darkened messily by prolific and curly black hairs; his socks were held up on elasticated suspenders; the tail of his shirt hid his thighs. What a romantic figure, he thought, and hurried to hide it beneath the conventions of clothes.

He returned to his wife, crossing to the window to fasten the shutters. 'Aren't you cold?' he asked her.

She placed the book down by the side of her chair and stretched luxuriously before answering. 'There's a good fire,' she said.

'It's a foul night.'

The doctor saw himself again, reflected this time in the window, before he closed the shutters. His beard had more grey in it than Mrs Goodchild had imagined, and his skin was paler. Against the dark evening and the damp window his face was as wan and disembodied as the moon. That's enough of that, he thought as he shut it out: a man can see himself to his own disadvantage only so often in an evening. 'I hope our guests don't get soaked.'

'What time is it?' asked Mary.

'Six.' He turned back to the room. 'Are you still reading that poem? You'll be able to recite it for him when he arrives.'

'I don't expect you to understand such things, but it is a very beautiful piece of writing.'

She was partly joking, partly mocking. He decided to change the subject. 'The boys are very quiet tonight.'

'Good,' said Mary. She bent to pick up her book, and as she did so her hair parted about her neck, revealing a soft and secret place. The doctor had an urgent desire to kiss her, but did nothing.

'I thought they might be excited,' he said. 'With the weather so foul and the thought of a newcomer.'

She did not answer so he looked at the fire. The flames bent athletically into the chimney draught: he looked for pictures there, and saw none. A coal balanced awkwardly on the edge of the grate, lit as with life from within, and then toppled on to the hearth, where it broke up in sparks and dust.

'Can I get you anything, Mary?'

'No, thank you.'

He leant across the hearth and picked up the poker. It was heavy in his hand, like a weapon. He tried to push the powdery coal back on to the fire, but it broke down into finer dust, so he prodded the fire and provoked sharp, wasteful flames.

'Stop it, dear, you'll spoil it.'

He put the poker down on the tiles of the hearth, where it rolled reproachfully back and forth before lying still.

'I'll make my rounds,' he said.

'I'm sorry, dear,' said Mary. She looked at him over her book. 'Have I been rotten to you?'

'It's all right,' he replied, surprised and pleased.

She stood up as he did and gave him a kiss. 'But it *is* a marvellous poem,' she said.

Clive Penn was governed by routines. From the sitting-room he walked to his surgery, which was also on the first floor, a high-ceilinged room that faced north towards the millstone grit crags of Grindlow Edge. Like the rooms he shared with his wife, the surgery was in the original building: Winfell had been built as a family home by a prosperous Sheffield coal merchant, and the war had killed his five sons. Now the doctor leased Winfell from the Blackhouse and Baldwin Fuel Company, and the coal merchant was dead of drink.

Facing north, the surgery got little light. Penn had had it painted white; sometimes he regretted it for it made the room feel cold. It feels cold now, he thought. There were a filing cabinet, a desk, and a pair of easy chairs. He crossed to the wooden filing cabinet and opened the top drawer. A fat wad of files greeted him, while at the back, hidden but usable, his service revolver made a grim souvenir. He ran his fingers over the files. Drummond-Whyte, Dyson, Fox-

Wesley, Gooch, Goodchild. The Goodchild file was thinner than the rest. He took it to his desk and sat down.

It was Penn's belief that memory and identity are much the same, and therefore the significance we attach to the arbitrary things that memory throws up is more deserved than would first appear. He held Mrs Goodchild's first letter in his hand. Sometimes, he believed, we remember things that have had no importance in our past but which, because we have now recalled them, will somehow affect our futures. He continued to sit in front of the letter, and remembered distinctly the day he had first read it. It had been cold. He had been sitting in his surgery, wondering whether to order a fire. It was morning. The walls of the surgery were mottled with reflected light or grey with its absence; the world beyond the tight rim of the window was sharp and clear.

He stood, as he had done that day, and walked to the window. The sun had cast the shadow of the house across the rookery and the summer trees; above the trees' plush leaves he had seen a faint full moon in a cloudless sky. He remembered the moon's pale disc, sloughing the blue like a florin beneath water. What makes us toss coins into water?

'Come in!' The maid brings in the morning mail on a tray and, putting it on the desk, tries a curtsy like her mother showed her, and leaves.

I go over to the desk, sit down. There are two letters, but one of them I recognise as a circular from a pharmaceutical company. I push it to one side. The other is more intriguing. If I've deciphered the smeared postmark correctly, it was posted in Gloucester. The handwriting is not familiar. Gussie's? A woman's anyway.

Mary bought me a sleek steel paper-knife last birthday, a precision instrument that cuts into an envelope like a surgeon's knife. Mary likes these modern things that fashion has stripped bare, and I like opening letters.

I swear silently: inside the envelope are two sheets of paper, held by a pin; I prick myself on the pin drawing them out. I look at my thumb. It seems undamaged, but when I squeeze the fleshy tip a bead of blood appears. I suck it off, annoyed.

I unfold the sheets of paper. The top sheet is a letter: the name at the foot is Sarah Goodchild; the address is Ashward House, Dollice, Gloucestershire.

I read the first two lines, and a kind of disappointment numbs me. A twofold disappointment: I'm disappointed for me, because I'd hoped the letter would be more interesting, but I'm disappointed for her. It takes a lot of courage to write a letter like this, to tell a stranger of these intimate fears, and yet there is nothing I can do to help. 'Dear Dr Penn,' she writes, 'I hope you will forgive me the liberty of writing to you out of the blue like this, but I need assistance, and your name was suggested to me by my good friend Lady Lougham. Ever since his return from France my son David has been unwell, and in recent months his health has declined. While physically he seems not unduly altered, his behaviour has, I am afraid, changed. He does not always seem to know what he is doing, or where he is, and sometimes, even in public places, he has been known to forget what is happening around him and imagine himself back in the war.' I admire the lady's bravery. In England they adhere with especial vehemence to Descartes's famous solipsism, *Cogito, ergo sum*, to the extent that those who cannot think are often deemed to have ceased to exist. 'Our doctor agrees that a change of scene might do him good, and I personally hope that expert care and the attention of someone who understood and sympathised with his condition might lead to some improvement.'

I lay the letter down on the desk and reach for my cigarettes. There have been many of these letters, but this one is more honest than any I remember. I would like to help; but the sanatorium is full. Symbolically, in tribute to her valour, I decide to forgive her the pin.

With automatic movements I select a cigarette and trap it between my lips. I flick my lighter but the spark does not catch on the vapour. I flick it again and the wadding holds up a purple flame. Idly I flip over the page to see what is written on the second sheet. A poem, typewritten. 'The Hour-Glass', it says at the top, 'by David Goodchild.'

> The words left are few
>   And the last sands
>   Mined from the edge of the glass
> Twist and fold, a heap, a cone,
>   As the hour-glass runs, runs out.
>
> Did Shelley see the world thus?
>   And the last sands
>   Mined from the harsh-grained stone
> Twist and blow, are dust in time,
>   As the hour-glass runs, runs out.
>
> The last words have been turned
>   And the last sands
>   Are blown across the ruined wastes
> Of palisades, of citadels and thrones
>   As the hour-glass runs, runs out.
>
> The last poet has been heard
>   And the last sands
>   Settle, are stilled, a heap, a cone,
> Soft and gold on the empty plain
>   As the hour-glass turns about.

It seems very good to me; although, as my wife would be the first person to acknowledge, I guess I'm not the best judge of poetry. I turn back to the letter again, looking for some reference to the poem, and find it between the two passages I read. 'I have included one of my son's poems. He has, I believe, some talent, and Edward Marsh has published several of his poems in his *Georgian Anthologies*.'

It is a pity the sanatorium is full. I like the idea of having a poet as a patient. Freud examined dreams, Rivers is sorting them out into meanings; perhaps Penn will unravel the psychopathology of poetry.

Besides, Mary has always wanted a poet.

The doctor put down Mrs Goodchild's letter, on top of a pile of correspondence that had accumulated since that first communication. Several letters had passed, in the intervening months, between the doctor and Mrs Goodchild. It was arranged that David should stay at Winfell not as a patient to begin with, but as a house guest. The house, already cramped, could probably squeeze another in.

Penn stood from behind his desk. He felt stiff, as though he had been sitting in one place too long, and curiously his thumb hurt in memory of that silly wound.

As was his habit, he again went over to the window. It was fully dark outside now, and only by cupping his hand against the pane to eliminate the glare of his electric lights could he distinguish sky and land. He left the surgery and went downstairs. He walked through what had once been the house's scullery and then, via a wooden passage, crossed from the house to the annexe. He saw the sudden cold of the passage fluffing the air before him with his breath.

The passage ended at a pair of fire-resisting doors. These led to a lateral corridor that ran the full length of the extension; at either end was a door out to the grounds. The annexe housed the patients and their communal rooms. The doctor turned left and walked between the closed doors of his patients' rooms and the wet windows that were shot with gravel sleet. Off the corridor at this end was the patients' common-room. He opened the door and went in.

The room was bright and cleanly lit, with electric light bulbs hanging from paper shades like the tongues of angular bells. Two crisply coated orderlies walked between the seated patients, offering glasses and pills. The orderlies' coats were ruthlessly white; the patients wore gentle shades, the tweeds and twills of gentlemen out of town. They did not look, at first sight, like men whose minds were lost; they looked like men enjoying a smoke.

Every evening Penn looked in on his patients in their common-room, moving through the cigarette smoke and the mouthing lips, wishing them good evening and talking of sport and the weather. Men with broken minds revel in quiet routines.

'Good evening.'

'Good evening, Dr Penn,' replied the patients.

He walked over to one of the orderlies and took him by the elbow. 'Everything quiet?'

'Everything's fine.'

He nodded. The patients sat in low armchairs and settees, their heads indenting the freshly laundered white cloths that protected the backs. Some were voluble, others reserved. He exchanged a word or two with each. Have patience with your patients, a wise doctor had once told Dr Penn, and he tried to adhere to this maxim.

'Corinthians won again I see. Your brother still playing?'

'He scored both goals,' was the proud reply.

'Good, good.' The doctor moved on. 'Lousy night,' he said to a seated patient.

There was no reply, and none expected. Penn pressed on. 'We'll have snow soon, I expect. It's already settling on the hills.' The man had eyes as soft and veined and pink with blood as some internal organ. These eyes flickered up at the doctor; it was all the acknowledgment he could demand. It was better than it had been.

There were fourteen patients at Winfell, sharing their disparate tragedies. The doctor smiled at them all, and left them to return to the house. The passage was as cold as before, but the scullery was good and warm.

At Sheffield Midland they changed platforms and changed trains. They had a long wait, nearly an hour, before the stopping train to Chinley that would take them to Grindlow. They drank Midland Railway tea from Midland Railway cups, and watched Midland Railway trains steam in and out.

The weather worsened. The rain tried to fall as snow, but the city air would not allow this. Smoky water traced its way down the walls, and the slummy hummock of Park Hill was a graveyard or a broken mouth. By the time they boarded their train it was almost dark.

Their new journey began by retracing their first: the Queens Road goods depot and the dull suburban stations. The character, however, was very different. This time the train always stopped. Heeley was small and dark, and wedged between lines of slate roofs. Millhouses and Ecclesall station was behind a great engineering works; advertisements for lung tonic and liver pills strutted in front of a quarry. Beauchief was surrounded by new houses, some of which were still being built, and shops that seemed rather older.

The wet darkness of the afternoon merged with evening, and evening spread out from the shadows. A tide of darkness at the pull of a mordant moon. Street lights came on: the main road was lit by faltering arc lamps that flickered an antiseptic blue; the side streets were lit by gas jets. Tramcars sparked their journeys, cascading electric rainbows through the rain from the upturned palms of their pick-ups. Their red tail lamps caught the jars in the chemist's shop, and the blue and gold was spun across by tricky scarlet glances. Or so it seemed, to David.

Dore and Totley station was bigger than the others. Over the road they could see large houses half-hidden behind trees, while directly opposite them was a line of almshouses, sprouting a sinister gothic tower, topped by a narrow spire. As David looked at this his random thoughts and perceptions began to harden. Having no paper, he treasured the ideas in his head.

Dore and Totley stands at a junction: left, the line goes south through the Bradway tunnel, the way they had come, and to Derby and beyond; right, and it is through the longer Totley tunnel and west towards Manchester. Their train forked right, down a long and scorch-sided cutting, and then underground. Overhead, unseen, the land changed: suburb gave way to pasture; pasture stopped abruptly at a dry-stone wall. After the highest wall it was moorland, and the snow was beginning to settle.

Leaving a tunnel at night is an aural, rather than visual, sensation. Immediately after the tunnel, the train came to a stop. A bored and bleary voice called 'Grindlow Halt' sporadically along the length of the train, and the Goodchilds climbed down. No one helped them. For a moment they stood, exposed in the gas light between their train and the walls of the station, and then the train pulled away, like a curtain opening in the cinema, and at once the sleet blew in and at them.

A man hurried over to them and grabbed at their luggage. 'This way,' he said through his scarf. They followed him over a footbridge, level with the signals, and then down the other side, to the eastbound platform and the waiting-room. They were shown in and they sat down. Their luggage made glossy puddles on the oilcloth floor.

'Staying in Grindlow?' asked the man who had carried the cases. He wore a railway uniform beneath a paraphernalia of comforts – scarves and mittens and balaclavas – he could have been a porter, or a station master, or both. He was the only person in sight.

'We're headed for the hospital,' replied Mrs Goodchild. 'But I didn't telegraph when they might expect us. Do you think we might get a trap, or would they send one?'

'Hospital?' His accent was rich and not offensive, when

you listened, thought David: rather like country smells. 'Do you mean the 'Ome?'

'Winfell?' asked Mrs Goodchild.

'That's the 'Ome,' replied the porter. 'That's the place I mean. The 'Ome.' He spoke with distasteful satisfaction, relishing the grubby word ''Ome' as a child might a naughty word. He looked curiously at David. 'He's nuts then?'

Mrs Goodchild gaped; David rather enjoyed the question. Before either of them could do anything the porter had bent down to light the Aga, embossed with a flourished 'MR'. He rummaged about in the opening and then drew out his hand to light a match. The flame diminished as it entered the hole and then it touched the oil burner. The small flame grew large.

'Wait 'ere and I'll see if anyone's 'eard owt about the 'Ome,' he said, and left them.

'How gallant,' murmured Mrs Goodchild at the closed door.

An hour passed, slowly. David ran out of cigarettes. The porter returned.

'No one's 'eard owt,' he said. His breath was furred with booze.

'Perhaps we could walk?' asked Mrs Goodchild.

'Three miles,' said the porter, discouragingly.

'I don't think I fancy that too much. If it's all the same to you, mother,' said David.

'Perhaps then someone could take us. Do you know of anyone going that way?' she asked the porter.

'There's a lad might do it,' the porter replied promptly. 'For a fair price.'

'Fine. Can you arrange it?'

'I reckon so.'

'Good,' she said, adding as an afterthought, 'What's a fair price?' She intended to give slightly more.

'Ten shilling.'

Mrs Goodchild looked directly at him. 'That's ridiculous.'

He avoided her gaze. 'That's price,' he said. 'That's what it'll cost you. If you want to get to the 'Ome.'

And how much to anywhere else? wondered David; once more he was reminded of gothic fancies, of the asylum on the hillside wreathed in mist, where beneath the full and werewolf moon, the mad doctor performed his perverted operations . . .

'Very well. If that's what we have to pay, then we will have to pay it,' said Mrs Goodchild with resigned tautology. 'But I feel I should complain to your superiors.'

'Nowt to do with me. It ain't my cart.'

'I suppose not,' she admitted. 'When can we leave?'

'When 'e's finished his doings.'

'And when will that be.'

'Nine o'clock.' The porter left them again.

They waited until twenty past nine. The porter reappeared at intervals, when trains passed by, but no one else appeared on the station. David elaborated his theme of gothic horror, including now a rough scenario in which mother and son are lured to a lonely station and to death. He passed this on to his mother.

'Oh, do be quiet,' she said.

'Have you any paper on you?'

'What sort of paper?'

'Something to write on.'

'There's some writing paper in the small case.' The Goodchilds had travelled light: Mrs Goodchild was intending to spend only one night away; David's possessions had been sent on in a trunk. She unstrapped a neat leather suitcase, rummaged about, and found some paper. 'Here you are.'

'Thanks.'

'Are you writing a letter?'

'A poem.'

She watched curiously. She had never seen a poem being written: she rather expected a flurry of activity and then the whole thing down on the page, as inspiration struck. Instead he looked rather like someone playing Kim's Game, she thought, as he sucked his pencil or added occasional lines.

He started with four lines then pushed them to one side. Once he added something, but later erased that. She presumed this was the beginning of the poem, but then he copied them down again at the bottom of the page and worked down towards them.

A cart arrived outside, and a hoarse urgent voice called from the rain, 'Hello! Anyone there?'

'Come on, David,' said Mrs Goodchild.

'A moment.' He looked at what he had written. There were three stanzas: he stared at the last and then, impatiently, crossed it out. 'It's not right,' he told her.

The rain had become steady downpour. A cart waited on the street behind the station. The weather seemed to bend down the ends of every straight line to a frown: the horse's neck hung as limply as its tail; the oilskin hat the driver wore drooped about his face; the porter, watching, seemed glad behind his thick and drenched moustache.

'Do you want your money now?' asked Mrs Goodchild coldly.

'Nay,' said the driver, helping her up. 'You'd best give it Jack. He's the one as wants your money, not me.'

The porter looked embarrassed but still took the note. 'I'll just look after it for thee, lad,' he said, recovering his composure.

The Goodchilds sat with the driver. Behind them the cart was empty but dirty: the driver's lantern found the grain of the boards outlined in mud. David wondered what the man had been carrying.

The rain seeped beneath their clothes, vibrated down by the movement of the vehicle. In its clammy coldness it was like waking from a fevered dream. They were tired and miserable by the time they reached Winfell. The driver helped them down, and carried their bags to the door. He would not take any money – 'I reckon you've paid enough' – and wished them a pleasant stay.

David rang the bell.

'Hello,' said Mary. 'Oh, dear. Aren't you wet. We've been waiting all evening for you to telephone us from the station; we intended to pick you up.'

The Goodchilds dried off before the fire in the sitting-room, while the Penns circled around them comfortably. Mrs Goodchild told them about the porter; Clive looked annoyed but Mary laughed. 'I expect he needs the money for his drinking,' she said.

'Do you know him?' asked Penn. 'Does he drink?'

'Like a lord, so I'm told. He's quite notorious.'

'I think a stiff letter to the railway company might cover that,' said Penn, adding, for his guests' benefit, 'My wife is a positive treasure-house of information of this sort. Fact of the matter is, she's good plain nosy.'

'I simply have a lively interest in humanity,' said Mary, with a smug patness that suggested she had said it before.

'But where she meets the people who tell her all she knows,' continued Penn, 'is a mystery to me.'

'When I'm walking,' she replied, dismissing the subject. 'But do tell me, I've been dying to ask,' she said, turning to David, 'Have you written any more marvellous poems recently?'

Penn opened his mouth to intervene. He sensed David's reluctance to speak. It was Penn's theory that the poetry might exhibit some of the tendencies of David's psychosis, and that therefore there might be a block about discussing it. Here he misinterpreted: David's reluctance was largely a cultured modesty.

His mother understood. 'What about the thing you wrote at the station?' she prompted.

'Oh, that,' said David. 'That's only rubbish.'

'Do tell me about it, all the same,' said Mary. Her interest sounded genuine, so he opened up.

'Well, I suppose I first thought about it when we saw the almshouses from the train.'

'In Totley?'

'I don't know. Perhaps. Anyway, that made me think about Trollope, and *The Warden*. Except that they're such ugly buildings, those almshouses you see from the railway. So that's rather what it's about. It's an ode, in a way: at least, it looks like an ode on paper.'

'You must read it to us,' said Mary.

'Oh no,' said David, positively alarmed. He seemed very young to her, wet and shy, wrapped in his towel like a child or a puppy. 'I couldn't do that. It isn't even finished.'

'Perhaps you could read it, Mrs Penn,' suggested Mrs Goodchild.

Mary looked quizzically at David, who paused and then felt through his pockets. 'I hope you can read it.'

'I expect I shall be able to.' She took the paper in her hand. It was damp at the edges. The poem was of three stanzas, but the last was crossed out. She read them all, regardless.

> In dread-owl night where hooded anguish prowls
>   The mind seeks signs to navigate despair.
> For myself, I cannot think of owls
>   Except I think of Goya, and the air
> Above the sleeping head a burst of bird
>   Wringing from the page; then, with this sign
>   I can make a pattern in my head:
> I cannot say that then my fears are cured,
>   For art's not palliative, it's paradigm,
>   But it at least makes measure of my dread.
>
> Some different place now, some Cathedral close
>   Where amber shadows patina cream walls;

    Some different mood, tranquillity, repose;
       A steady bell's grave note, the gathered shawls
    Of those who go to prayer, the marvellous spire
       Balanced in the air, and, undefined
          But tangible, the presence of the Lord.
    To people the Cathedral we require
       A subtle, undramatic art, a mind
          Affectionate, ironic and assured.

    I think perhaps the art we love the best
       Is that best fills imagination's needs,
    And while it is didactic to suggest
       Criteria for art, it most succeeds
    Where it fits my thoughts, where some sublime
       Connection helps establish what things mean;
          I think of Goya when I feel morose
    And bats fly from the dark; at other times
       A different mood prevails, I am serene,
          And Trollope peoples each Cathedral close.

'I like that,' said Mrs Goodchild when Mary had finished. 'It seems very sensible.'

David sneezed loudly. 'Sorry,' he said, blinking.

'I think that must be a cue for bed,' said Penn. 'It's wrong of us to keep you up on such a night.'

'It has been very pleasant just sitting here and feeling human again,' said Mrs Goodchild graciously.

'Thank you. I'll just show you to your rooms.'

The doctor left them. Their rooms were opposite one another across the landing.

'Have a bath, David, before you go to bed, dear,' said Mrs Goodchild. 'Wash away the journey.'

David agreed. He had a towel in his case; Dr Penn had indicated where the bathroom was. He walked along a short corridor towards it.

A white panelled door was open. In the shadow David

could see the firm cold edge of the bath, and the different texture of a rug on the floor. This must be it. He found a string and pulled: electric light revealed a crisp winter scene, icy glossy surfaces that shone. Sharply folded towels on a metal rail reminded David that, despite appearances, this was a hospital. David shut the door and pushed across the bolt. The bath itself was of a cream enamel, and stood on archaically clenched clawed feet. David ran the water. One tap was hot and shone; the other was cold and dulled with condensing droplets.

He sat on the side of the bath. The water splashed its length and then climbed between narrow walls. He lit a cigarette and blew a plume of smoke into the steam. The smoke was of a different texture, was thicker yet more vivacious, and remained true to itself in the thin vapour that hung over the water. The sound of the antiquated plumbing knocked loudly. He watched the mixing of smoke and steam. The narrow confines of the bath were first a trench and then a grave. Hot water whistled from the faucet.

He left the bathroom door open as he went, and his walk was almost a run. He carried his belongings bunched in his arms, and after he had closed his bedroom door he leant against it, in relief and fear. His mouth became awkward with breath, and his chest was tight. His mother heard the decisive click of David's lock and looked out of her room. She could hear water swarming into the bath, and see steam busying itself at the bathroom door. She went to investigate. Through the bumbling steam she saw fat waves that licked the brim of the bath. She hurried in and turned off the taps: the buzzing of stinging water ceased at once. On the water the sodden constituents of a sometime cigarette unrolled messily. Mrs Goodchild rolled up her sleeve, scooped up the cigarette distastefully, and reached for the plug-chain. The plug jerked free, and the water began to twist away. New noises began.

David had moved to his bed. He sat down with another

cigarette to his mouth. He did not light it at once. These were the doctor's cigarettes.

He was shivering. The water ran from his bath. He heard it go. It gurgled through the neighbouring pipes, and was the sound of blood in frightened veins, the sound a soldier hears. David took his steel lighter from his pocket and flicked the wheel: a delicate flame occurred, shimmering in his shaking hand. He brought the flame towards the tip of his cigarette and drew breath through the paper tube; he had to clasp both hands about the lighter to steady it. The flame ducked, sucked towards the cigarette; the tip glowed vermilion as he soothed himself with smoke. I have two minds, he decided: one is empty, one is full. My full mind does not work.

The first of July. This does not feel like victory. We are to be the third wave. The first two have already gone. I watched them. They have not gone very far.

Things are not as they should have been. *The artillery will use shrapnel shells which will cut through the wire*, they said. *The bombardment will inflict heavy casualties*, they said. *The survivors will be too demoralised to fight*, they said.

I have seen whole companies die. The machine-guns' bullets slice them, a grim harvest before the reaper. I have seen men stare with wonder as they learn how thin is skin, how fragile life. I have seen men's minds react to the death of all their friends, and one I saw, in no-man's-land and quite alone, calmly removed the bayonet from his rifle, put the barrel to his mouth and pulled the trigger. The top of his head came off.

It must soon be our turn. We wait. The men keep low for fear of shrapnel or straying bullets. I watch as much as I can through my patent trench telescope.

Ahead, the major gets to his feet, waves us on. Bent double, like miners, we move along the trench, around a corner. I think I am frightened: my mind is full of the ricochet of straying bullets. We are doubled up, at the double, doubling back along the trench. Such are the geometrics of a war, I suppose.

Stop. Think. We must wait now. The company in line abreast. At ease. Cigarettes are lit beneath cupped hands, sheltered from the sun as though from rain. No one bothers to speak: life is trivial enough without admitting it. A whistle sounds down the line.

Suddenly the major is blowing his whistle; we are all blowing our whistles. In line abreast we mount the parapet; in line abreast we climb over the sandbags; in line abreast we move across the field.

In line abreast we die.

The man closest to me pulls me down with him as bullets whine overhead. I lie still, winded and stupid. There is no verb for the sound of too-close bullets. Perhaps something to do with the bowels or bladder would suit. If I am lightheaded it is because I am alive. I lie flat for a while, until the bullets have all gone, and then turn to thank my saviour. He is not a pretty sight. There is a bullet where his nose was, and his brains slop down his cheek.

There are bodies all around me. It was far easier to see what was happening from the supply trench than it is from here. I am confused now, and worried; I shut my eyes and count. Only one thing is really clear: to stand would be suicidal. I count to twenty-five, and stand.

Nothing happens. I do not die. It is as if the war, mistaking me for dead, has moved away. I step forward, and then break into a run. I'm alive. Smoke gusts back and forth across my line of vision. Ahead I see trenches and, surprisingly close, a machine-gun on a salient. I turn towards it. The smoke hides it and reveals it: it is a coy machine-gun. I am almost upon them before they see me, and their grey uniforms seem almost turquoise in the summer. They exclaim at my approach though, and the barrel swings around. I suppose I ought to kill them but my mind is not quite right: I think I might embrace them instead.

The barrel trains upon my chest. I see the tightening of his eye before the tightening of the trigger. Then comes the blast, the agony of light. Like dark spots on the sun, figures move across the glare. They are the machine-gunners, gracefully expanding and exploding. There is no up nor down, just the vivid colours pulsing in my eyes. The colours clear to a thinner film. I look about. I am lying on my back with my head stretched back painfully. The machine-gun lies near me, twisted and wrecked. A slow understanding like a dawn seems to warm me: a stray shell has hit the machine-gun post. I close my eyes again. I think that I should rest now.

> I have been drilling the men today.
>
> A cold wind blew
> As I told them what to do.
> It was a dismal day.
>
> I told them what to do
> When the whistle blew.
> The sky was grey.
>
> I drilled them through and through
> While the cold wind blew.
> It was a poor display.
>
> I drilled them through and through
> And then the whistle blew.
> It was time they earnt their pay.
>
> I told them what to do
> But the Germans drilled them too
> In their thorough German way.
>
> It was a dismal day.

CHAPTER TWO

It had snowed overnight, and the charabanc was slow to start. They gave Mrs Goodchild a coffee while she waited, and watched the driver wrest the starting handle round. The windows steamed up as they watched. Eventually the driver was successful. The motion of his wrist was transformed and magnified into rattling convulsions of the vehicle; when the convulsions had steadied to a judder Mrs Goodchild walked out, was kissed by her son, and climbed aboard, helped up by the driver.

They found an awkward gear and moved away. The cold clenched itself in David's toes as he waved. The charabanc passed out through the gates, rutting the snow and smearing it with oily shadow, and disappeared. They heard it long after it had gone.

David went back in. The Penns were waiting for him by the open door. 'I must do my rounds,' said the doctor. 'But I'm sure my wife will entertain you. I'll have a chat with you this afternoon, David.'

'Thank you.'

The doctor went below the stairs to the scullery and the annexe; Mary and David climbed to the first floor and the sitting-room.

'Tell me,' said Mary, 'all about poetry.'

'I don't know that I can.'

'I'm sure you are being too modest. I've read some of your poems you know.' She opened the door to the sitting-room. He followed her in. 'I think we had better have a fire,' she said.

'Which have you read?' asked David. He felt bashful.

'The ones in *Georgian Poetry*.'

'Oh.' She waved for him to sit down, and he did, sinking into the floral cushion comfortably. She sat opposite him and looked at him intently.

'I do love to read a lot,' she was saying. 'Modern books mostly – I do love modern literature, don't you? – but I so rarely get the chance to talk to anyone well informed. It's such a treat to have you here, you can't imagine.' She laughed, prettily, putting her head back to show a long white neck.

'Thank you,' he said.

'So we must talk about literature. The two of us.' She smiled at him encouragingly. 'Mustn't we?'

He smiled back.

'Tell me, David – I can call you David? – tell me, what was the last book you read?'

He thought for a moment. '*Moonfleet*.'

'*Moonfleet*? she said. 'The children's book?'

'I suppose it is a children's book,' said David, as if he had not thought of this before. 'I rather enjoyed it.'

'I meant the last, real book.'

'Oh.' He thought. 'I'm afraid I don't read all that much any more,' he said apologetically.

'But you must,' she argued, and then a thought struck her. 'Or do you only read poems?'

'I do read poems,' agreed David.

'Richard Aldington?'

'I'm afraid not.' He tried to smile again. 'I think I met him once. Most of the poets I read are dead.'

'In the war?' she asked, and then, remembering his condition, wished she had not.

David did not seem to mind. 'Longer ago than that, actually.' The conversation was becoming a game; David was enjoying it at last.

'Don't you like modern poetry?'

'Not much.'

'You disappoint me,' she said, trying to make it sound as if it were not true. 'But never mind. I shall educate you.'

She went to a bookcase by the window and selected a handful of books, carrying them back high against her chest as women always seem to do. 'Here,' she told him.

She lay them out on the floor in front of him. Their gaudy dust jackets, blocked with formless print, were not to his taste at all, but he nudged one with his foot. 'I've read *A Room with a View*.'

'Did you enjoy it?'

'It was all right.' He looked at the other books. 'I've met this chap. Funny looking fellow with a moustache and a big nose. Met him at Garsington, the Morrells' place you know. He didn't say much, actually. More sort of glared.'

'He's a genius.'

'That's what he seemed to think. His wife was nice, though. German. Always flirting.' David toed the next book. 'Tut, tut. *Eminent Victorians*. Shouldn't this be under lock and key? What if the servants should read it? You know what's happened in Russia.'

'You're mocking.'

'Perhaps. I haven't actually read it myself. I wouldn't want to.'

'You mustn't believe all that you've heard about it, you know. It really isn't so dreadful a book. It's quite nice to General Gordon.'

'I'm not scared of being corrupted. It isn't the book I object to, it's the author.'

'Have you met him?'

'Often, more's the pity.'

'How is it that you can meet all these people without ever reading their books?'

'You don't have to read a bloke to meet him, you know. In fact, I usually find that meeting them makes me quite antipathetic towards their writing. All writers are liars, you know. They make their living telling fibs.'

'That can't be true!'

'Why not?' David looked at his knees and wished he had a cigarette. 'There's nothing wrong with telling fibs, of course. Very few people, writers or otherwise, do anything else. At least writers by and large do it well.'

'You are going too fast for me,' said Mary. 'How can you say that everyone tells fibs? That can't be true?'

'Why not?' he asked her. He felt older than Mary now, more powerful. 'Describe this room,' he suggested. She looked at him. 'Describe this room,' he said again.

'Four walls; a ceiling; a floor. A door over there. A window. Will that do?'

'More,' he urged.

'A window-seat. Two chairs in front of the fire, matching. Two people in the chairs. One of them is talking, the other one listening. The talking one is female, the listener is male. He is about five foot ten inches tall, with fair hair and blue eyes. He has a moustache. She is about five foot two inches tall. Her hair is dark. She sometimes thinks that she is quite pretty but not at the moment. Will that do?'

'You haven't said much about the room,' he pointed out. 'Just the people.'

'Well, they're more important than the room.'

'Not to an architect. Or to a detective if there were a murder. The architect would want to know what sort of window-sash or skirting-board or whatever there was. The detective would probably be interested in blunt instruments, paper-weights and pokers and things.'

'That's not fair,' she realised. 'You're going to accuse me of lying by omission. It would take ages to describe everything in the room. No one could do it.'

'Exactly. No one could. And even if they did, you'd just have an inventory, not a room.'

'So how do you describe the room?'

'You can't. You can't describe anything. You just pretend you can by lying with lots of conviction. That's probably why people write poems, come to think about it. The rhythm and the rhyme disguise the omissions.'

'It's like talking to Clive,' said Mary.

'Clive?'

'My husband. Dr Penn. He talks like you sometimes. Not about poetry, but about other things. He analyses everything too.'

David felt rebuked. He was silent for a time and then asked, almost timidly, 'Did you enjoy my poems?'

'Yes,' she said, generously, forgiving him anything.

'Then,' he said, calculatingly, 'It's true what I said. Meeting the author can be a big disappointment.'

'No,' she said firmly.

'Yes.' He sat back in the chair. 'The biggest invention an author makes is himself. The self in the poems or the books, I mean, the reasonable, ordered narrator who tells you the story. Strachey in real life is the foulest, most mean-minded swine it has ever been my misfortune to meet, but I am prepared to bet that the character that comes over from the books isn't like that.'

'That's true,' agreed Mary.

'You couldn't let me have a cigarette?' asked David, shamefacedly. 'I ran right out yesterday evening.'

'I should think so,' said Mary. There was a wooden box on the mantelpiece. She picked it up and offered it, open. He selected one. 'That was a bit of a change of subject. Strachey to cigarette in two sentences.'

'I like talking to you,' said David. 'I feel I've known you for a long time, yet we only met yesterday.'

'And that,' Mary added, 'sounds like a line from a bad novel.' And then she laughed again, showing off her fine neck. 'Perhaps I remind you of your mother.' David laughed too; when he looked at Mary he knew it was not that.

A fussy, high-toned gong called them to lunch. The

dining-room too was on the first floor. 'Typical,' said David. 'I've just lit a cigarette.'

'Tell me, David, about yourself. What do you remember?' asked the doctor. 'Can you tell me about the very earliest thing you remember?'

It seemed cold in the surgery, despite a healthy fire. David thought.

The fair is noisy and bright. Machines whirr and fizz through an undergrowth of painted legs, and the legs flick back and forth across the light.

Someone wins a prize – is it me? My father? – and I take it home. It is a glass vase, cheap and beautiful. It is my prize.

We get home. I want to drink from it. My father will not let me. It is dirty, he tells me. It is mine, I must tell him, but I cannot make the words. He lectures me and I cannot make the words so I cry.

That must be my memory, his glass voice and the vase. And I cry, and I cry, and I cry.

'Good,' said the doctor. 'Would you like a cigarette? That was excellent. Now, you're probably wondering what the point of this is. Yes? Well, in a way so am I because I won't know what is significant and what isn't in your memories until much later. At the moment we're trying to find out as much as we can about you, that's all. If you feel that there are things you'd rather not talk about you can avoid them if you like. You can even leave – you can leave of your own free will if you like – there's no Reception Order keeping you here. But I hope that you'll do neither of these things. I hope you will tell me everything. We're working together at this. If we're to make you better we must trust one another completely. We do trust each other, don't we?'

David took a cigarette. My first since lunch, he thought. The doctor took one too, and flicked his lighter. Nothing happened. He tried again. David offered the doctor a light.

'Thank you.' The doctor put his barren lighter away. 'Shall we carry on?' David lit his own cigarette, and nodded.

Mrs Goodchild sat on the train, and she too thought of the past. The train was stationary between lines of scrubby hawthorns: amber liquid froze beneath the hawthorn boughs; snow blossomed on the branches and mocked May. There was an emptiness inside her she could not name. It was nearly hunger.

She could not get rid of the thought that David had been taken away from her for good. She thought of previous partings. David dressed in blue, knees scrubbed red beneath his shorts, on his way to private school; David off to Eton, grown up and handsome, with his Norfolk jacket and brave smile; David going to war. But none of these partings, so it seemed to her then, as she sat on the train, had felt so final as leaving him at Winfell. When he had gone to the private school he had cried; when leaving for Eton he had been as grown up as possible, but had still managed to whisper, 'Can't I stay here with you?' before boarding the train; they had never been so close as when he went off to war. But this time, leaving him with the Penns, there was not even the memory of his grief to give her comfort.

She remembered his birth.

It had been a hard birth, a long swollen delivery. Sometimes she had not believed that it would happen, nor that this child could ever come from her. Sometimes she had not even wanted it to happen. Let the child stay there; it is what we both want.

Between the regular bouts of pain she was calm and

lucid. She could see the midwife frowning. Try harder, said the midwife. You must try harder. Sometimes the clock struck the hour. You must try harder.

The pains filled her until relief could only be to burst. The last pain, the greatest, was a spasm and a split. My God, she thought, as viscera seemed to flood down on her legs, I have torn in two. The ritual slap and the wail did not interfere with her peace. There was no feeling of achievement. She was only glad that it was over.

Afterwards, remembering that relief, remembering how glad she had been to have emptied herself of him, she felt unnatural. Is every birth such a mess, she wondered. No wonder we are always at war.

The doctor asked him about his school.

I struggle with Virgil. *Forsan et haec olim meminisse iuvabit.* Perhaps one day we shall be glad to remember even these things. It is a wet day at Eton in June. It seems unlikely, frankly, that I shall be glad to remember this, whatever the future might bring. M'tutor has set me four hundred lines of Virgil for tomorrow. It seems unlikely that I shall manage that, either.

College is full this afternoon, because of the weather. We crowd into Chamber. I'm in my stall, pretending to work, and I can hear Jacques and Fiebo messing about in Fiebo's stall next door. Jacques, who can be a terrible fool, is lighting a cigarette: Fiebo is soft on Jacques but still has the sense to object. 'Don't you like it?' asks Jacques, sounding rather hurt. 'I thought you'd approve of the languid air it gives me.'

'I don't,' says Fiebo. 'And the air isn't languid, it's putrid.' Rather good that, for Fiebo. He must have heard it somewhere before.

An urgent knock on the side of my stall tells me that the Captain of Chamber is coming in. I pass the knock on to

Fiebo in his stall, and am rewarded by muffled squeals and the sound of towels fanning the air. Doing my bit for them I climb on to my washstand and open the high window; the Captain sees me and calls:

'Hey, you. Goodchild thingummy.'

You know my name perfectly well.

'Come here, will you.'

All right. All right. I'm coming, aren't I?

'Now listen, runt.'

That's good. I'm nearly as tall as you, and will be taller when I'm your age. I say nothing. 'I'll be wanting a wash later . . .' You mime washing your face: you are pretending that you fear I won't understand this word 'wash' '. . . so be a good chap and fetch a chap a can.'

This is not a request. I have been here too long to fag for you, but you can still twist my ear. You do this now, in case I have forgotten. I haven't. You call this 'pinning the pinna', or sometimes, 'consulting the auricle', but you think it hurts more than it does, so I am winning. You tighten the twist and release me; I make an elaborate pantomime of agony, and then go.

I collect the kettle from the wash pipes and carry it up to New Building. It is heavy: it bangs and slops at my knees as I haul it with both hands. You room is in Passages, and you have it to yourself. Naturally, though, you aren't there, and I have to wait outside.

When you arrive you show me in. Your room is clean and piled with books, cloth-bound scholarly books with spines that have frayed. I fill up your washstand and wait. 'What are you waiting for?' you ask, and reach for my ear again. On an instinct that could earn me a thrashing I put my hand up and catch yours. I pull it away from my head. To my surprise you yield; our hands move together through dusty air, and then we stand, your hand in mine, facing one another. Whole moments are wasted this way.

Suddenly you tug, and your hand is free. You reach for my head again, but completing my surprise you do not pull my ear. Your hand roughs my hair; your face unfolds into a grin. 'You're a fairish sort of fellow,' you are saying. 'Look after yourself, what?'

Your teeth are white. Your eyes are blue. I have never been so happy.

The doctor rested his pen on the open clasp of his notebook. 'I take it there was nothing . . . nothing more to this relationship.'

'Good Lord, no.'

'You would tell me of course if there was? You already know you can trust me.'

'You can trust me too. Nothing came of it. I'm quite normal, even if I do write poetry,' added David.

Penn looked steadily at him; David felt compelled to explain himself further. 'You asked me for a memory of school and I gave you one. I don't know why I chose that.'

They sat in silence. They both knew this was not true. David knew exactly why he had told the doctor this; the doctor thought he knew too. But their reasons were not the same: Penn looked for some deep-seated urge, however undeveloped, towards inversion and homosexuality; for David, the scene with the Captain was an image of trust. He had put himself into the hands of the Captain as keenly and willingly as he now committed himself to the doctor. David was very passive in many ways. Even now, when he resented the doctor, the habit of depending kept him calm. The doctor unclipped his pen from his notebook and, in his cursive hand, made a misleading note. The interview continued.

A bottle here on the hill; a bottle in the wardrobe at home. And both of the buggers are empty, thought Jack Brough.

He looked down moodily at the railway line below him. It ran with thin strokes of silver on grey along the length of the valley. The spark-tossing trains had melted through the snow about the track in irregular lesions. The track passed the back of Winfell. Jack Brough thought of the couple he had shown there the previous night. Ten bob? Not bad. Not bad when it came from the lousy Home.

Jack Brough loathed Winfell. He loathed what it was and what it stood for. Officers got shell-shock; privates got drunk. Jack Brough had been a private.

Even here there's the same bleeding difference. Them and us. Rich and poor. Officers and other ranks. Red lamps and blue.

It's bleeding true. The officers go in under the blue lamp, get the special treatment, the whores who aren't worn out and toothless. Some of the ones we get, they've serviced the entire French army before we get a look in. Serviced it since Waterloo. Go in the red lamp and the biggest fear's that they might peg out on the job.

It's a real circus this. There's half the battalion here. Three hundred of us and a dozen of them. What happens if they get full up, that's what I want to know. I mention this, with a laugh, to the bloke as stands in front of me, but he's Chapel and he doesn't want to know. In fact, seems to me that if I bait him a while longer I'll be able to get him right out of the queue: he's a might green round the gills already; if I tell him a thing or two about what he might catch he'll be off, I reckon.

I don't get the chance though. There's a rush and a push and he's gone, leaving me right at the front of the queue. If this was a proper brothel I'd be able to take my choice now; at this place I'll be lucky if they find me one can stand. The madame waddles into view: it's my belief she's a bloke dressed up; she's got a red dress and an orange boa, and she looks like me Aunt Daisie on a Bank Holiday. Her face could kill at forty paces, and there's a rumour going round that they're hoping to use her to open up the Second Front. But worst of all is, she's the advert, she's the best bleeding looker they've got.

Someone's finished quick because she's showing me in. I'm trying to get my flies unbuttoned before I get in. If I'm not hard before I meet my bit I know I never will be. The madame shoves a curtain to one side. There's a girl in a dirty dressing-gown sitting on the bed, but she can't be mine, she's under fifty. More than that, she's under twenty, and slim and soft and lovely. She doesn't look like she belongs here at all, except for her expression. Her expression says she's a whore. Her expression says she's bored as hell.

So does the dressing-gown. She shrugs it off mechanically and lies down, me with her. This is all right though. I'm lying here with my best parts in her hand, and she's bringing me in, bringing me in. Then I'm sliding in the softness and dampness and dancing my arse like a steam pump.

Afterwards I'm done and happy. I make to kiss her but she shoves me away and gets up. I wish I could bleeding paint. I'd paint her now, slipping the dressing-gown back on, the oil lamp by the bed making half moons of light to cup her breasts, and her flat belly beneath licked by a curl of white that's like a feather and a flame. But I can't paint. She shifts me out and the madame leads me away. I go out a different way from the way I went in: they don't want us as have done to tell the new customers what we've caught.

There's a fire back at the camp, and a few bottles of cheap red wine. The wine tastes like vinegar, but my balls have started to itch now, like a straw mattress at midnight, so I drink it all the same. I might as well love that girl as love anyone, I decide. I've no one else to love. I fall asleep.

Grindlow, below him, was a scatter of dark roofs melting the white, and the mouth of the tunnel hung slack. The snow balanced on upraised branches and a harvest of ice hung below. He turned to climb higher up the hill. Sometimes, as he passed between the trees, his shoulders brushed off thick wads of snow.

He stopped again, turning away from Grindlow to look along the length of the valley. Smoke rose steadily, unflustered, from the houses and villages along the valley sides. The nearest smoke rose from Winfell.

The Home's red roofs slipped their snow as the house warmed up. The snow fell in folds of white on white. From where he looked the annexe was virtually hidden behind the house and the rook-shot bare branches of the trees; the house looked virtually unchanged, like the family house it had been. Suddenly Jack Brough uttered the short deriding laugh that was the sound of anger. They're playing bleeding snowballs, he thought out aloud: they're bleeding playing bleeding snowballs.

They ran and jumped in the cold delirious snow. The doctor made the first ball and threw it into the pack. It burst on a patient's ear. He made a second and a third and threw them too; by the fourth the battle was joined. Snowballs rushed from man to man, to fracture in silent white puffs as they struck. A chase of snow happened, a flurry. Dark shapes of motion crossed fields of bright white; the balance and fall of the snow confused them; they were numb in their fingers and toes. Each of them was almost glad, and light-hearted enough to pretend joy. It did not matter that they were insane. Everyone is insane in such snow.

Afterwards they went in and dried off. They felt tired and pleased. The doctor felt tired and pleased. He liked his patients to enjoy themselves, he liked to reintroduce them to activity. The hard and truth-denying snow had seemed a godsend, obliterating the world as it is and had been. Dr Penn stood by the door at the end of the annexe corridor. Behind them an anarchy of footprints showed where they had played.

David looked at the mess in the snow. He had not been outside, but had remained in the quiet room he had, thinking. He wanted to write a poem.

What is snow? Frozen water, but water that has frozen in a special way. Water that is frozen, yet is not ice. A poem is like that; it is an idea that has turned into a crystal of delicate beauty; it is something that can transform a landscape or smother a man, yet something so fragile it can be moved in a single breath. David stared from the window at a poem of hills and trees. He saw muscular grey clouds flexing at the rim of the world. Cold rooks patterned the sky. Their heavy wings flapped big and small, flickering up on the clouds. Darkness conspired on the house and marched from out of the east. David dressed for dinner. The landscape sank through dusk's grainy water and reached the night sea. He sat at his window, watching and smoking. The world became different again; it sang to a different poem. Now the sky had turned blue, and the snow wore the colour of clouds. A chirurgeon-barber sliced moon, stranded in a patch of anaesthetised sky, healed the white earth.

David, in a white tie, heard the dinner gong. He went down the stairs to eat.

CHAPTER THREE

I T SNOWED AGAIN that night, after David had gone to bed, and this softened and blurred the marks left by the snowball fight, except in Leonard's mind. Leonard, in his bed, crouched in a mustiness of sheets, could not sleep.

Where he lay, with his knees pulled up to his chest, was too hot, and his pyjamas grew fat and cumbersome with his sweat, but he knew that if he were to turn over, the thin cold of the rest of the bed would chill him. He lay still therefore as the warm pillow rubbed raw his ear and his mind drifted in winter. His eyes were open; his eyeballs darted like those of a dreamer. He remembered Caporetto, and the snow.

It doesn't take long for them to discover. There's always somebody guesses. Sometimes I think they must have an instinct for telling: those Italian boys, the ones who dropped their trousers and mooned themselves at our train, they couldn't have known. And yet, it seems to me, as they gave that derisive, provocative gesture, that they did. And what about the soldiers, only yesterday, queuing to be deloused after our journey? From the laughter that entered their voices just after I'd gone by, I could tell that they knew. Or tonight even, when Cleyton struck me?

It is cold tonight. I look down from the redoubt and see the river Piave edged with ice. It isn't dark in the valley, despite the night: the snow seems somehow to store up the daylight and leach it out slowly through the darkness. But it is cold. It seems much colder than it did last week, when the battalion was in Flanders, although there was snow there as well.

I wish I could keep my secret. They all despise me so. It's true: every one of them despises me. The Italian boys with their tantalising plum-smooth bottoms; those soldiers at the delousing station; Cleyton tonight. Once they know my secret they hate me.

The valley jerks into extra light. For a moment I am confused, and then I realise that a star shell has burst overhead, and is floating down on its parachute. The snow glows more brightly, and the valley is quite brilliant with incandescence. The river shows up as a greasy slick, and the snow on either side is broken by humps and earthworks. They affect me strangely, like freshly dug graves. Beyond the river, unexpectedly, the Austrians are climbing from their trenches. It looks like the Resurrection; the battle has restarted.

I duck down into the redoubt and try to see the situation from my periscope, but the frost has got to it and the ice is on the inside of the lens. My stomach mutters inside me. I blow on the periscope in an attempt to warm it up and that just makes it worse. I knew it would. Things conspire to show my fear. Now I have to climb back up to the top, face the battle, and report. And I know I cannot do that.

The battle of Caporetto continues without me. It is in its second week now. Eight days ago the Italian front line was the river Isonzo, but then the Austrians broke through, at a town called Karfreit on my captured Austrian map, but which the Italians call Caporetto. I remind myself of these details to get away from my fear. The Austrian push forced the Italians back to the second river, the Tagliamento, and there the Italians surrendered or deserted. I wish I dare do that. I wish I dare join the plum smooth Italians on their mountains. Instead I came by train, moved in with many thousand French and British reinforcements to hold the

Italian line. We travelled a long time, crushed into the smelly coaches, and when day broke the Italian boys lowered their trousers at us.

As I crouch down one of the machine-gunners who shares the redoubt is climbing the wall. I do not know these men: the old battalion has been broken up, and I am with strangers. Even the gun is a stranger, a captured Austrian weapon with a fat water-cooled barrel. The man climbs to the edge of the redoubt and looks out. Like one with a fear of heights I cannot watch another take this risk. The very thought of the view spread before him makes me shake inside: my stomach quails, guts guttering like a flame.

Even when I am not looking I see this man fall back. The bullet has made a small hole in his forehead, and a larger one where it passed through his left ear. He lies at the foot of the redoubt, and blames me for his death.

The other man is shaking me, mouthing words in a difficult tongue. 'Give ... us ... hand. Work ... traverse.' He rams the end of a belt of clips into the machine-gun and feeds it through as I pull the trigger. I tap the gun steadily along a two-inch traverse, mechanically counting the clatter of spent cartridges while I wait to move the gun's aim.

The mechanical rhythm of the gun, and of my part in pushing it round, quells my mind. I feel myself becoming gun, as fed as anything by the fat belts of bullets. The noise we make is a chant. Daka-daka-daka. I am more machine than man, minded by the loader next to me. Daka-daka-daka; two-inch traverse; daka-daka-daka-daka; two-inch traverse.

Distantly there is the squeal of a whistle, suggesting something is happening, a counter attack by our troops. I wheel the machine-gun again: daka-daka-daka.

These are French. I hear their cries of lust and despair as they move past our position. One falls, wounded, over the sandbags. His helmet, daka-daka-daka, rolls from his head. It is a ridge of steel over curved protecting sides. It is a penis, limp over steel balls.

Daka-daka-daka.

The English troops follow. I push my gun back over the line of the traverse. Daka-daka-daka: I spit bullets into the night. Madly, I climb up to the edge, where there is only exultation in place of my secret fear. The gun, of its own momentum, carries on traversing the field. It lines up on the advancing British troops who have drawn abreast. It picks places on faces and chests.

Daka-daka-daka. They fall. Daka-daka.

The gun jams.

I leap back into the redoubt. My mind is frantic. I take hold of a man and shake him, demanding to know why he didn't stop me, but he is dead, and his head lolls to one side. I turn to my loader. He must have known. But like me his thoughts are awry.

Without thinking I climb from the post. I run towards the dead men. The snow is pulp beneath me. When blood is hot it sinks through the snow, but colder and older it only smears the surface. I reach the bodies. I have some silly notion to apologise. I kneel by the first corpse I find. It is my brother's.

Minutes pass in cringing terror before I take another look and make sure. There can be no doubt. This man was once my brother. My throat is full of my love for him, and then it pours in a stream of thin bile from my mouth, slimy and warm in the snow. Somebody knocks at my door. I cannot turn to face my dead brother.

'Good morning, Leonard.' It is the orderly who brings me my tea, as he does every morning, but there is no time for him now. I close my eyes against my brother and move to the next body.

'Leonard?' asks the orderly. I shall not be disturbed. The second corpse is face down, and while the orderly calls out my name, I turn it over. 'Leonard? Are you feeling well?' I was right. This, too, is my brother.

In the corridor there is shouting and the sound of running feet. It does not worry me now. I sit on the bed and I weep, for my secret fear and my brothers.

Mary was first to wake. Her husband lay beside her: his deep breaths pulled at the air and sifted it out through slack lips. For the second morning in a row, she found herself waking to the unfamiliar brightness of the morning as reflected off snow, dappling the ceiling of her room. The light suggested it was time to get up, and the entry of a maid confirmed this. The girl carried a coal scuttle, went over to the exhausted fire, bent down and swept out the grate before arranging new coals on the top. Mary traced the girl's routine by the sounds that it made: the whispering of the stiff brush; the dull empty knock of the coals; the patient striking of matches until the fire had taken. When the maid had gone, Mary got up.

The fire burnt low and did not yet warm the room. The doctor had insisted, on principle, that his own fire should be the last to be lit in Winfell: Mary thought rude things about principles. She crossed her arms before her and hugged herself a little warm, then gathered the hem of her nightdress to her waist and hurried it over her head. Her nipples were proud from the cold. She dressed quickly.

Her husband awoke, and looked to see her clipping her brassière behind her back. A year ago he would have remarked about this, 'Best part of the morning and I missed it,' as she tucked her soft breasts away, but now he turned away to read the alarm clock. 'Is it really that time?'

It was a characteristic of their marriage that Mary, who loathed the mornings, should get up first, while Clive, who really did not mind them, waited in bed and complained of the time: it was as though, in an effort to accommodate the other's opinion, they had accidentally exchanged their views. Mary went to the bathroom; her husband stayed in bed. It was only when she returned that he got up.

Mary waited for him as he washed and dressed, and they went for breakfast. David was already waiting, with the newspaper open before him. They exchanged good mornings. 'Anything in the paper?' asked the doctor.

David leafed through. 'Cambridge beat the Corinthians. The Corinthians will play Public Schools tonight, too. They'll lose again, I expect. They're not the side they were.'

'A shame,' said Penn. 'Anything else?'

'Sugar has come off the ration.'

'Excellent.'

'And about time too,' said Mary.

'There's a war in Lithuania.'

'Isn't there always?' asked Mary.

'The Irish crisis continues.'

'Doesn't it always?' asked Penn.

'And that's about the lot.' David folded the paper and put it down on the table. 'Oh yes, it will snow again today.'

'Hasn't it always?' asked Mary.

After breakfast Penn left David with Mary and started on his morning rounds. He visited the patients briefly first.

'Doctor Penn! Please! Here!'

He strode up the corridor to his right, away from the common-room and the usual route. 'Yes?'

'It's Leonard, doctor. He's not well.'

'What's the matter?'

'I don't know. He's right badly.'

Penn reached the orderly, who stood in the doorway of Leonard's room, keeping his eye on the patient and the corridor. He looked in, and was relieved by what he saw, for although Leonard had obviously been sick – the stench alone said that – he was sitting on his bed obviously much better. 'He's been sick,' he told the orderly, unnecessarily and rather abruptly. He did not like his routines to be broken.

'Aye,' said the orderly.

'Come on, Leonard,' said Penn. 'Feeling better now are you?'

There was no response. The doctor went into the room. 'Come on, old fellow. Snap out of it.'

Leonard's eyes were fixed on the wall opposite. They did not move. 'We'd better get him cleaned up,' Penn told the orderly. There was apology in his voice.

'Aye, sir,' said the man. He coughed.

'Yes?'

'Well, sir. I'm the night orderly like, and well, my missus'll want me back. I'll be late enough already.'

'Yes, of course. Send someone else along to take over though, can't you?'

'I'll fetch the sergeant.'

'A good idea.' The sergeant had once been in the BEF, and had somehow always been a sergeant. The doctor could not imagine a time when Sergeant Horton had ever done anything other than tell others what to do. He turned back to Leonard: too many others in that sentence, he thought. It saved him worrying about Leonard.

Come on fellow, he willed. Come on. We've known each other too long for you to break down on me now. Come on. I thought you were getting better. Come on. 'What's the matter, old chap?' he asked.

The doctor sat down by his side, avoiding the drying dregs on the bed. They sat like that for a little while; Penn could feel the bed shaking. He reached over for the blanket and put it over Leonard's shoulder to stop him shivering. Leonard took no notice of this for a while, and then moved a quick hand up to clasp the blanket at his throat. That's better, thought Penn, although Leonard still shivered and still did not speak.

'We'll leave him a little while, I think,' he said, ostensibly to the orderly in the corridor. 'Poor Leonard. He must be hungry by now. And we've got bacon and kidney for breakfast too; you know how much Leonard loves bacon.' Penn turned round to see if Leonard had moved at this; he hadn't. In a lower voice he added, 'Could you keep an eye on him, do you think?'

'If you want me to, sir.'

'Good.' Penn looked back at his patient for a last time. 'You'll let me know if there's any change.' What an institutional, ineffectual thing to say, he thought.

'Yes, sir.'

'Good. I don't think there should be any problems.'

The orderly rubbed the back of his neck. 'Reckon I could handle him if there were.'

'I hope to goodness it won't come to that. There's no reason why it should. He's a peaceful fellow by and large, you know.'

'Yes, sir.'

'It's as well his room is right at this end of the corridor. Keeps things rather more private. None of the others need pass, I mean. Do they know what's going on?'

'Only that he's poorly, sir.'

'Good. We'll keep it that way, shall we? Some of them are fairly impressionable; we don't want them all to stop talking to us.' He smiled and the orderly smiled back. 'I'll leave you to it then.'

He was late so he rushed through his rounds, but he was thorough and all got done. He did not forget to say a good morning to each of the patients. Nor did he forget to send a chair to make the orderly in the corridor more comfortable.

A visit had been arranged for that morning: one of the patients was to receive his wife and children. The doctor had set aside an hour, and Mary's sitting room; the wife arrived late. She was small and pretty, and when she climbed out of her chauffeur-driven Rolls-Royce (her hands hidden in a fur muff) she had looked so smug he had wanted to kick her.

It was an unsuccessful meeting. The patient failed to recognise his own children; the wife seemed only to be looking for evidence of insanity. She addressed her husband exclusively through the doctor, speaking of him in the third person as though he was entirely cut off from her (and therefore confirming that he was), and referred frequently to the fact that, 'He's not getting any better, doctor,' despite Dr Penn's muttered warnings.

She left after twenty minutes; she did not think she would be coming back to visit, as it was too painful. Her face she compressed primly into a formal and shallow mourning: she looked like the unexpected inheritor at the funeral of an unknown great-uncle, whose sense of propriety demands a semblance of pity. Mary, watching the dove-grey car pull up the slushy drive, said 'Bitch!'

'Pardon?' said Penn in surprise.

'I'll bet she has another man.'

'Really?'

'She wanted poor Dennis to be mad, so that she can divorce him. I bet that's the way it is.'

'You're probably right. Poor Dennis.'

For richer, for poorer, in sickness and in health, thought Mary. 'I love you,' she said.

He was surprised, but rather pleased, at her words.

His good mood faded. He went back to see Leonard, but nothing had changed, save that there was now a litter of cigarette ash on the floor beneath the orderly's chair. Leonard remained just the same.

The doctor returned to his surgery. He felt depressed. Leonard, Dennis, the rest. Trapped in their own messes. He ordered lunch, then returned to the annexe, where he gave instructions that Leonard should be cleaned up, dressed, and taken to the common-room. 'Make him feel a little more loved, poor fellow,' he said.

Damn this, he felt.

After lunch he read what he could about fugue, for he was worried about the severe nature of Leonard's withdrawal. There was a knock on the door.

'Come in.' It was David. 'Hello?'

'Our appointment,' reminded David.

Penn checked his diary. David was right: God damn. 'Come in and sit down. You want a cigarette?'

'Thank you.'

'Perhaps you'd . . . ' He stopped. What were we talking about? 'Perhaps you'd like to carry on from last session.'

'London?'

'That's right. London.'

'You're as bad as your wife, she's already asked about that.'

But she's really interested, and I'm not, thought Penn. At this moment, his thoughts continued (while David began to speak) I'm afraid you're only a distraction, with your petty neurosis and your poems. David continued to talk, thinking himself back to the remote pre-war world. Idyllia, Halcyonia; Penn found himself thinking back too. I'll give you this, David Goodchild: you remember things clearly and well.

I would not like to say what Percy Lewis thought he was doing when he painted the curtain to look like a piece of raw meat. I can only assume he was commenting on the cabaret we'd find behind it. Certainly, at this moment, and with those hideous red and white camels around the border, painted by that young Jew, Epstein, it's like being inside a Bedouin stomach rather than a nightclub. I don't know how much longer I can stay here anyway. Too much cognac, for one thing, and too many girls from the Slade for another. The Johnlets, drooping violets who would, the most of them, benefit from a wash. Some could do with a shave too. Too much cognac. There are eight stages to tying a dress tie, thank you.

Henry calls for champagne. It is all Madame Strindberg will serve. It tastes extraordinary, but familiar, at once. Of vanilla, mainly, I think. The first stage is to cross the two ends in front of you, right over left, and then to pinch them together with the fingers of the left hand.

The girls from the art school have formed a circle. They hold hands and swing into the tables. Henry points out one of them, a plump girl in a curious costume apparently held together by a large *diamanté* brooch. He says she is his sister. Then you take the right-hand end, which is now on your left, and pull it behind where the two ends cross. Straighten it with both hands. His sister? It must be time we left.

I look for someone I know, to point out to him and redress the balance. I can't recognise the people we arrived with, even, which is odd.

Welbo says he wants to leave, though dear old Jack is far too happy. He's dancing with a waitress, lucky swine. It's a well-known fact that the average waitress is far more willing than any number of girls from the Slade, despite the latter's flaunting. I'd rather make a waitress than an art student too: less chance of an inquisition afterwards. Welbo, meanwhile, as befits a peer of the realm, has deposited the contents of his glass over another customer, and is making unsteadily for the door. I grab Henry and we move towards him. Even in the Cave of the Golden Calf, I suspect, customers will complain at being drenched. So much for bohemianism. We sneak out, crouching low to avoid the suspicious glances of the denizens. We pretend that we are Boers.

The next step is to tuck the ends through this loop to form the bows. Start from the right. The fresh air makes me realise how drunk I might be. Push through, double back, repeat. I am drunk as a skunk on a bunk, I tell Henry, and he says he is jrunker.

Jrunker, nonshense. I am inebriated to the point of utter collapse. I am intoxicated. I am under the influence. I am in my cups. I am tipsy, tight, squiffy, sozzled and soused. I am stinking, boiled and canned. I am soaked, oiled, pie-eyed and pickled.

At this point Welbo hiccups his dinner – a decent one at the Savoy – all over Bloomsbury. Jrunk ash a lordj! Jrunk ash a lordj! yells Henry, while the . . . fourth? fifth? . . . Lord Welborough grins insipidly through glossy lips at us. Finally you straighten the tie, balancing the two bows until they are equal.

A djentleman, I was once told, is a man who can put on a tie after two full bottles and with a cigar in hish hand, but we have run out of cigars and so I can't be a djentleman. Thish annoys me, particularilarily shince I have tchaken off my tie onshe more simply to prove my point.

I think we shall head for dje Café Royal.

'Doctor, please, quickly.' The door was opened and an orderly stood there, panting and trying to speak. Smears of blood shocked his coat. He looked, David thought, like the messenger from a Greek tragedy, but before he could remark on this to Penn, the latter was on his feet.

'What's happened? What's happened?'

Penn rushed past the orderly and down the corridor. David, abandoned, gazed back beyond the bloody starched white coat and into his dangerous past.

Leonard had been sitting in his chair for so long that they had almost forgotten him. Cigarette smoke filled the room. Somebody snored gently in the low light. Cards rippled from pattern to pattern. Dominoes chattered and snapped.

Snapped.

Stop it! Stop the guns that killed my brothers! Stop it! The guns crackle on the board; the dominoes are black tombstones that talk with the voices of guns.

Stop it!

Enraged, I rush at the players, sending the dominoes flying. The air is thick with their black squares, blocking the light like bats. I have hold of one man. I hit him. He crumples his face before the blow hits, and my fist only consolidates his pain. I hit him again.

I reach for the other. He has backed off screaming but I shall have him yet. I shall have him yet, unless too many try to stop me. I can hear already the short firm sound of his bones. His nose is mine, and his jaw.

Too many try to stop me. I realise I must break away. I must go to the mountains, where the plum smooth Italian boys hide. I must tell them about my secret, and about how I murdered my brothers. They will understand, and will turn their sad bottoms to the moon. I push towards the window and the hills, and make a dash.

The glass explodes messily, painfully. The panes split and cascade but the metal frames just bend. I pull at them and force them further apart, embedding sharp pieces of glass in my hand. Now there is room to escape.

I jump through the window and run. The blood from my hands burns holes through the snow. I knew it would. They will follow me by the red trail. They will trace me by my blood. I press my hands to my chest to staunch the flow, but the blood pushes through at my wrists and won't be stopped. I turn towards the mountains, where the snow is still unbloodied. The smooth curves of the snow hills entice me.

They are behind me, the haters. I hear voices that yap and bay like hounds. I hear them over the noise of my gun, the sharp daka-daka that rips through my brothers. The snow is heavy and thick, and must be shoved aside with each step. I am not running any more. I am wading. My feet no longer push the snow. I am stumbling.

The snow is soft by my sides but pressed solid beneath me. I can no longer hear the battle. Just random shouts, distant and pleasant, like calling birds. The Italian boys are coming down from the mountain. My brothers climb up to greet them.

David was still in the surgery, and Orpheus sang.

> The afternoon is tired and balmy
>   (The bullets are only anxious flies
> Fizzing in the air); the army
>   Settles back and shuts its eyes,
>
> Forgets the vermin and the Huns
>   And the Staff Corps' latest blunder
> (The restless beating of the guns
>   Down the line is summer thunder;
>
> The bodies out in no-man's-land
>   Relax and bask in soothing sun.)
> We sit and talk and crouch and stand
>   And sleep and write our letters home.
>
> The men write postcards. I can't guess
>   Where they get these postcards from,
> Embroidered with a martial crest
>   And 'Loving Greetings From Your Son',
>
> Or a portrait of the King
>   Above the caption 'God And England'.
> (The postcards open up their wings,
>   Like butterflies on their tame hands.)
>
> These postcard colours seem too bright
>   And cheerful for this cheerful war.
> Their hopeful messages are trite.
>   And yet, they seem to say much more
>
> Than my long impassioned letters.

Do not look back, Hades said, but that was not possible. Orpheus was a poet: he had nowhere else to look. He reached the very mouth of the cave and turned and looked back at Hell. He could not help it. There was blood on the snow-white coat. Eurydice vanished. He let the maenads tear him apart.

Penn found him on the floor.

'Come on, old chap, come up to bed.'

The doctor felt an excess of sympathy course through him. He picked David up from the carpet. 'Come on, up to bed,' he repeated. David staggered to his feet. 'It's all right. Leonard's all right.' David had never met Leonard, did not even know who he was, but he was glad Leonard was all right. The maenads had left him; now he was mostly tired. 'Come on, fellow, come on up to bed.'

Dr Penn supported David to his room and helped him on to the bed. This is all I need, thought the doctor. 'I'll send someone to look after you,' he said.

He hurried downstairs and across the annexe. Mary was there already. 'Is there any change?' he asked her.

'I don't think so.'

Penn drew one of the hovering orderlies outside. The man he chose was Sergeant Horton. Sergeant Horton could be relied upon.

'Our guest, Mr Goodchild, has had a collapse. He's in the spare bedroom in the house. If you could go up and look after him I'd be very grateful.'

'Sir.'

'And don't mention it to Mary. She's enough to think of without anything else, and anyway we don't want to embarrass the poor chap.'

'Very good sir.'

The sergeant walked away, his feet loud on the linoleum. Penn straightened his back and re-entered Leonard's room. He had work to do.

The doctor saved Leonard's body; he could not save his mind. They patched up his jagged wrists and watched him all that night, while David slept in the spare room, beneath the skylight and the gaze of Sergeant Horton. The following day there was a change-round. David was given

Leonard's old room; Leonard was taken to an asylum north-west of Sheffield. They did not trust Leonard with cutlery, so he drowned himself in his soup.

CHAPTER FOUR

Between the house and the annexe, and bordered on a third side by the connecting passage, was a patch of ground described euphemistically by Mary as 'the kitchen garden'. She had ambitious plans to cultivate this plot, but so far all that had been done was to push aside the rubble left after the building of the annexe and to erect a stone bird-bath in the centre.

Sometimes she sat in the warm scullery, looking out over her prospective garden, and planned what she might plant. She read with delight from Culpeper's *Herbal*:

Loosestrife is good for all manner of Bledyng at the Mouthe and Nose; Orach cures Headache, Vvanderyng Paynes, and the first Attacks of Rheumatism; Uiper's Bugloss is an especial remedie against bothe poisonous Bytes and poisonous Herbes; Eglantine is excellent for Apolecia or falling of Haire.

Now it was winter, and the snow had hidden the couch grass and reduced the nettles to insubstantial stakes. The bird-table too wore a lid of snow. Everything was tamed and domesticated; the snow tended her garden. She went outside and brushed the snow from the bird-table, and left stale bread on the ice.

She watched the birds squabble from the scullery. She saw tits that flashed blue and yellow, and the unctuous plumage of starlings; dramatic blackbirds with orange beaks grubbed daintily between the sparrows; a robin, amused at the fuss, perched at one side with its jaunty head cocked.

Of all the birds she loved the robin best. She loved the way he remained aloof from the quarrelling, artless sparrows. She loved the way he puffed his red chest at the cold. Especially, she loved his trust. When she walked out to replenish the bread on the table the other birds all flew away, but the robin stayed to watch her, regarding her amicably with his round metallic eyes. She sang as she broke the bread.

> The North wind doth blow
> And we shall have snow
> And what will the Robin do then, poor thing?
> He'll sleep in a barn
> And keep himself warm
> And tuck his head under his wing.

It was pleasant in the scullery, and busy. Since her husband had moved David into Leonard's old room she had not seen so much of her poet. Still, she was glad he was to stay at Winfell. Orderlies went back and forth between the house and the annexe, fetching medications or blankets, and travelling in gusts of cold air. Without David to talk to the days seemed longer. The annexe faced back across the kitchen garden. Sometimes she looked there for her robin.

David was getting better. His mother came to visit him, the week before Christmas. They exchanged presents and greetings, and then she left again, returning to Gloucester and her home. She was finding an increasing need to attend the church; she was looking forward to the Christmas service in the cathedral. Her cab took her from the station and along Northgate Street; she asked the driver to detour, and to take her through College Court. They stopped outside the house of the 'Tailor of Gloucester'; a recent black plaque announced that this was the tailor in Beatrix Potter's story. Winter sunshine cast long shadows. Across the court were the pretty, patient houses of College Green. The trees were bare. She asked the driver to stop. To her right was the cathedral, carved and skeletal, the colour of rich bones. Its tower threw a band of shadow across the lawns. She was determined not to weep. With a word of apology to her driver, and the instruction that he should wait, she entered the cathedral.

A choir was practising, hidden from her behind the wooden screen and the finely pitched organ-pipes. Boys' voices vaulted the air. Her feet slapped the flagstones as she walked to a convenient chair, knelt, and placed her hands together. The knuckles were white on her steepling fingers, with the suggestion of age and of bone; her fingers echoed the rhythm of the Norman piers that held the arching veins and ribs of the roof. Dear God, let David get better. Dear Jesus, let him be well. The choirboys' song seemed to her as a wind: it caught up her thoughts as the wind might do smoke, and whipped them away and dispersed them. She cringed before the bass notes of the organ. The ceiling soared above her and the air was vibrant with song. Dear Jesus, let him be well. Her fingers shifted, gripped one another. She prayed hard through the storm of the choir, hoping to make herself heard. Dear God, let David be better. The music suddenly stopped.

Dear Jesus, let him be well. Her thoughts, as firm as a statue, as pure as a bone, echoed dizzily in her head and through the stones.

The snow turned to slush and then froze. On Christmas Eve the roads to Sheffield were blocked, and the company laid on a special train to ease the load of shoppers and travellers from Grindlow and the Grindlow Valley. Jack

Brough was not pleased. He was meant to finish work at six-thirty; he didn't finish until eight.

By then it was bitterly cold. The disturbed snow on the path out to Grindlow broke noisily under his feet. Puddles cracked into tilted planes of geometrically arranged ice. The ice made tumbled roofs and walls in the footprints and the puddles, like ruins in old excavations. He walked through the trees that isolated the village from its station, and stamped the snow from his boots before entering the public house.

The bar-room was crowded.

'A whisky and a beer,' he said as he pushed through to the serving hatch.

'Both for you, are they?' asked the woman behind the bar.

'One's for Father Christmas,' he told her.

'You know the rules then. No chasers.'

'It's Christmas Eve!'

'Law's law,' she said, reasonably.

He muttered something about the Defence of the Realm Act. 'I'll just have the beer then,' he said. 'Tha'd better make it two. Is that all right?'

'There's a law 'gainst treating too,' she pointed out.

'I'm not treating. I'm drinking. There's not a law says I have to queue every time I need a drink is there.'

She jerked her head up and let it drop again. 'Hark at thee, Jack Brough.' She pulled two pints from the ivory handled pumps. 'One and seven, please.'

'Thruppence a pint it once were,' he said habitually.

'Aye. Happen it was,' she said, turning away from him to drop the change into the till.

He went over to a bench by the fire. The heavy scent of wet straw and drying farmers made him wince. He drank down one pint and returned to the bar.

'Two whiskies, love.'

'You again?' She served him his two whiskies. Defence of the bleeding Realm Act. Don't make me laugh. He drank one off at the bar and returned to his chair with the other. Gives a beer more push, he decided, pushing a whisky down after it.

The bar was full, but Brough sat alone. He made steady trips to the serving hatch: two whiskies, two beers. He poured them down. The heat and the pain were like love. There were cries for young Froggat to play the joanna. 'Silent Night'. The ceiling was the colour of nicotine fingers. Light reflected in his glass: in strips of length up the sides, and in bubbles of decaying brightness at the brim. 'It's snowing,' said someone, rejoicing. 'It's snowing for Christmas.' The door was open and cold air fell in, sprawling at his feet like a drunk. He shifted his legs. 'Does tha want another?' He lifted his bleary glass but the question passed over his head. The piano competed ineffectually amongst the conversation. Snatches of music and words slipped into his mind through the noise and the booze. 'She never!' He caught the mordant tones of 'In the Bleak Mid-Winter'. 'She bloody did!'

The room filled up with smoke before his eyes. Glasses grinned their curved mouths at him. His eyes were bright. He grinned back. His waking dreams were of broken nights, and sometimes he dreamt of sleep.

Crowded room. Marks and scuffs of shoulders on the distemper.

'I've come to take the shilling,' I say.

'In line,' jerks a jerk with a jerk of his head.

The oath: one softly whispered so the jerk won't quite hear it; the next out loud to God, King and Country. Red hands on a morocco Bible. Walrus moustaches. Tommy Atkins signing up.

'No time for that,' says the jerk. He's no longer a jerk though, I find: he's a Non-Commissioned Officer and I'm an Other Ranks. He doesn't say what there's no time for. He doesn't need to. There isn't time for anything.

Into the back of a truck. Self-conscious, and then

disappointed no one cheers. Madam, do you recognise the sacrifice I'm making? No? No, you wouldn't, silly cow. Posters on the side of the truck. 'Take Up The Sword Of Justice.' 'Women of Britain Say – Go.' That one certainly did! Silly cow.

Rattle of springs and teeth. Smell of oil and teeth. Bloke offers us gaspers from a tin: he'll not do that again; there's eighteen of us. More rattle and bad breath. Flapping canvas sides and the only view we get is backwards. The world moves away from us. Like freedom.

Changes of gear. Gates close behind us. The truck slows to a noisy halt. The tailflap flops. 'All out!' Clothing issue – 'You can't have that – it fits' – and beds. Shouting sergeants. Hup-two-three-four to bed.

The sergeant-major is Welsh. He's also a bastard, but you can't blame his father for that: even in Wales there's a law against marrying pigs. Right, gennelmen, though calling some of you lousy little bastards gennelmen maybe a little bit of arteestic licence on my part, today we're gownadoo Bayonet Drill, and this here is a bayonet in case you've been wondering what it was you've been carrying around next to your balls, while this here is, for those of you without the benefits of an education is, or so I'm reliably informed by Riley aren't I Riley, is a rifle with, at one end, the narrow end, the end the bullets come out don't they Riley yes of course they do you see he isn't just an ugly face he's also nearly human, but not quite, at this end the business end is a hook and a hole and at the count of three, wait for it, I'll tell you when, I tell you everything, don't I Riley you four-eyed Irish git, don't I sunshine, at the count of three you will insert said hook and hole thusways, got that, thereby attatching bayonet and rifle soes that you can kill people with it, one, two, three, missed that didn't you, I'll say it again ONE TWO THREE that's better and now you're all ready to charge at those dummies there, no not Riley though I can see how you made the mistake come on sunshine you first that's it run,

run, run, NO, stab it what are you, get it in there, you a frigging virgin or something get it in.

BASTARD!!!

Trained and on a train. Night departure, like we're ashamed. Dover smells of old fish and old seaweed. The troop ship smells of old soldiers.

Twenty odd miles they reckon to Calais, but we've puked so much over the side the distance must have doubled. Two officers sit with us, talking warfl warfl. A funny thing about officers: field marshals always have lots of chins; junior officers none. Like, when the good Lord made officers, he gave them the right number of chins between them, but the army cocked up the distribution. This wouldn't surprise me: you should see the boots they've given me.

Then it's a train. 'Change at Y,' says an officer.

'Why?' we reply.

'Not "Why", "Y".'

'That's what we're asking.'

He draws a letter in the air. We nudge one another. 'He's making rude signs at us.' 'No, it's a dirty picture.' 'Shall I send him a message back?'

'Look chaps,' he says. 'Please . . . '

We've won. We settle back into our seats. It won't be such a bad journey. Dawn breaks over flat France. The houses are different and I can't say how.

'It's not like home, is it,' says the bloke next to me. 'Like, the houses look the same but the windows are different, and the chimneys are the same but the roofs are a funny shape, and the land looks the same but the fields aren't the right size.' I look at him. He's young. He's right. We're a Derbyshire regiment, Pals Brigade. I offer him a cigarette. Least we can do is be pals.

'Sir?' A chap leans across, talks to the officers. Voice low, confidential. 'Where're we going?'

Sharp, irritated, not to be drawn, 'I've already told you.'

'I don't mean where we change trains, sir. I mean, where do we get to in the end?'

'Death,' says a voice, confidently. 'Death.' Heads crane to look. A veteran, no older than us but with less kit and better fitting clothes, rolling an experienced cigarette. He grins. 'That's where you're heading, lad.'

'You've survived,' I tell him.

His grin widens. '"The bells of Hell go ting-a-ling-a-ling for you but not for me,"' he sings. I envy him his balaclava and mittens and certainty. I don't often envy people, it's not my way. But Christ! I envy him.

> The bells of Hell go ting-a-ling-a-ling
> For you but not for me,
> And the little devils how they sing-a-ling-a-ling
> For you but not for me.
> O! Death where is thy sting-a-ling-a-ling?
> O! Grave thy victoree?
> The bells of Hell go ting-a-ling-a-ling
> For you but not for me.

The train gets to a station and we get off.

'You've six hours,' says a sergeant at the station. 'Which means if you're not back in five hours I'll take your balls for a baccy pouch. Understood?'

'Yes, sarge.'

'Louder.'

'*Yes, sarge!*'

'Right. You're in a town now known, for purposes of security, as "Y". Don't anyone ask me why: the answer's "Why not?" Which leads neatly to my next point. Get tempted by the thoughts of France, do we? Fancy a fling on the Folly Bergers? And why not? *I'll tell you why not!*' he bawls unexpectedly. 'Because there are things you can catch here what they've never heard of back home. One poke in this place and your prick'll be lying in the street in front of you before you've said *Mercy boocoo*. Got that?

You'd better not get it, sonny, else you'll know about it!' We laugh. He seems to expect it. 'Remember. You're here because, in its infinite wisdom, the British Army has put you here. You have nothing to do because the Army has left you nothing to do. You are allowed to wander the streets because Staff say that you can. You are *not* here to get pissed. You are *not* here to get laid. And woe betide you if you miss your train, because then I'll have you here, to myself, when all your mates have left. *I'll* enjoy that; *you* won't. Got that?'

'Yes, sarge.'

'Louder.'

'*Yes, sarge!*'

'Right. Di-i-smissed.'

The officers walk off together talking about architecture. We hang around the platform. Uncertain of one another or where we are. We're only a group because we sat on the train together. No one wants to take the decision.

Eventually enough people get fed up with the station for us to leave and walk around 'Y'. The five hours seem to stretch to Christmas. We slowly realise we're bored silly.

The people I'm with are as much fun as head lice. I'm the only railwayman here: the rest are all miners and clerks; the miners stay together – I'm stuck with the bloody clerks. We're meant to be Kitchener's New bleeding Army? Don't make me weep.

A new train, smaller, Frog, takes us out of 'Y'. Standing up. Playing cards standing up. I think about helping my luck along, but it's too cramped to cheat, what with everyone looking down your neck and up your cuff. I've lost near three tanner now, bleeding hell. Still, my luck has to change soon.

It does. The train stops. We get off, line up, are shouted at. There's no platform, no town. We've travelled the full day now. The dusk shows us nothing, tells us nothing. We march.

> The bells of Hell go ting-a-ling-a-ling
> For you but not for me.

It gets darker. We walk along a broken track. We can't march here. It's all rutted with feet and wheels. Some of the wheels remain, broken on the side of the track like bits of old boats.

> O! Death where is thy sting-a-ling-a-ling?
> O! Grave thy victoree?

There are buildings along the path from time to time, but there are no lights in the intervals and we don't stop. I'm getting tired. We're all getting tired. The singing stops. The song isn't right any more. It gets quite dark. I can feel myself working out what I'll be saying, some day, back in Blighty: 'I'm not a superstitious man, don't get me wrong, but we all of us – the whole company, the whole battalion – we all of us shut up on the road to . . . ' To wherever.

You don't sleep that good your first night in a trench. Nor your second, neither. The whizz-bangs are the worst, and the rats. The rats get every place. Old soldiers who are younger than me tell us we've got it worse than most, because this is the bombardment before the big push and our guns are at it day and night. Least, they say it's our guns: they all sound the same to me.

Daybreak. It's June, it gets light early. But there's no cheery sound of bird-song, oh no. We have to shout to make ourselves heard over the barrage.

It's a communications trench this. The parapet is held up by wooden pilings, and the pilings are resting behind picks and shovels. Something is coming up: I mean that two ways, too. Like, one way there's something big going to happen soon, and another way I think I'm going to be sick.

I've never had much time for prayers, or for serious thinking. I've never believed much in anything save getting on, getting by, getting laid. But I'm learning one important thing now, right now. I'm learning what there is to know about Time.

Time's a bugger. When I'm drinking, which isn't as often as it should be, I reckon I can control Time. That's what I drink for. That's what drink does, it puts you in charge of Time. So a drunken moment lasts me hours or a drunken hour no more than a moment. So that I can go right back in Time if I want. But who in Christ's name would want that?

Sober, Time's the boss. That way it'll shove, push, smack and then leave you stranded. Look how it got me here, just look. Recruiting office, camp, boat, train, march – shove, push, smack here I am. June's already July; I'm standing in a trench by the Somme, waiting for an attack, and Time has left me hanging here by my balls now.

My gasper burns down so slowly it'll decay before it's been smoked. There's a beetle tumbling in the wet earth at the sides of the trench. The sun is warm and useless. No one has spoken since the war began. I try to tell a joke but nothing happens, so I pretend that I was whistling and can't even whistle. No one has spoken since the war began, and the war has lasted for ever.

Hey now, lad. Stop it. You're not the type for this sentimental clap-trap. But I still can't think of a joke. And I still can't bleeding well whistle.

Suddenly, roughly, I'm pushed to one side. A corporal leads a stretcher party back from the front line. A line of canvas stretchers covered with lumpy, bloody blankets. Each has a mess of a man. Some of the blokes in our company throw up. For some reason it doesn't get me like that. I'm just curious. Most of the casualties have no bandages, nothing to hide their wounds. You can see right in: there's more in us than in a rabbit, and what there is seems darker, but its the same sort of tangle of tubes. Quickly I find I'm ill after all, and squat to choke up my rations. Even before I'm upright again we're on the move though. It's happened; it's begun.

Creeping along the trench. Past bodies, grim with flies that burst up at us. One trench meets another and we turn left. There's a bramble at the top. It probably survived by pretending it's barbed wire. It's blossoming early; I get this sudden urge for a blackberry. I wonder if it'll still be alive while September.

I wonder if I will.

There's a whistle, but we haven't ever done this sort of thing before. Not for real. We nudge each other and look around, but the officers and NCOs climb the parapet, and the sergeant swears himself blind. No one wants to go, and no one stays behind. Like sheep going over a cliff. The parapet is sticky with blood, and other things even less nice. My fingers rub my palms mechanically, like a fly washing. 'Advancing across no-man's-land in full pack,' say the orders. 'Dressing from left to right.' The shells were meant to cut the wire; I can't even find a gap in the smoke. We only carry on because we don't believe this: they can't really mean us to die like this, in the smoke; can't they let us at least see who is to kill us? The smoke thickens and palls. I tread in a dead man's head, and then I'm sick again.

Get him out. Anxious unconcern surrounded him, vague faces that look down. *He can usually hold it better'n that*. He heaved his head up on his hands and placed his elbows firmly on the table, disturbing his recent vomit. He looked about him. He was lost, in time and drink; the familiar magic of the alcohol was wearing off.

He stood up, swayed, and righted himself. He wiped the back of his hand across his mouth and tasted his own sickness. It was sharp and stung his throat.

'I'll have another mild and a whisky,' he said, clearly. There was a murmur of approval from the bystanders that cheered their reluctant interference for them. *He's his sen at any rate*.

The landlord looked across from the serving bar. 'Not

in here you won't.

'What?' asked Jack Brough.

'You've had your belly full. Get off home with you. Sleep it off and a merry Christmas.'

'You think I'm drunk?' Brough was incredulous. 'Me? On the watered down fizzy-pop you serve here? Drunk? You don't know the meaning of the word. Drunk? I'll bleeding show you drunk. You just watch, aye, you, thee, just watch. Drunk. I'll gi' thee bleeding drunk. Ah've a bottle of whisky at home, bottle of whisky. I'll show you bleeding drunk. You watch, thee. Bottle of whisky, straight down. I'll show thee bleeding drunk!'

He stumbled to the door but held his dignity as though it were balanced on his head. His back was straight and his chin was high.

'Merry Christmas!' called a voice.

'Ah'll be back!' he called.

The people in the bar nodded. Oh yes?

It was warmer than it had been. The trees were shrugging off their snow now. Hard icy branches pattered the settled snow below. Icicles dropped testily. The ice in the streets retreated to the edge of mushy puddles. He passed the Christmas churchyard; his bladder was swollen and uncomfortable. There was a service going on. He slipped in through the lich-gate. The bright and recent electric light bulbs lit the church comfortably and decorated the gravestones with many-hued light that passed through the leaded stained-glass. He stopped by a gravestone, unbuttoned his flies, and washed the remaining snow from the name of 'Martin Preskey, Of This Parish'. Beside him as he pissed a window cast its pattern and he made out, on the unbroken snow in the church's lee, the projected design of the Remembrance Window, elongated and undulating but still quite clear. Christ, clad in all his glory, his head surrounded by a comb of gold, blessed a kneeling khaki soldier. When Jack Brough looked up at the window the inscription was reversed; spread out in the snow at his feet the inscription was miraculously corrected. 'For The Fallen 1914 – 19' he read on the snow, 'Lest We Forget'.

The choir sang its praises. Jack Brough watched his miracle. The music clambered higher. The descant rose above the melody: it sang choirs of angels, sang them in exultation. Jack Brough fixed his eyes on the image of Christ and stepped forward. His shadow fell across the Saviour.

They forgot Jack Brough in the tap-room. The sawdust absorbed his vomit; tobacco smoke disguised the smell. They sang carols. As a Christmas concession, at midnight their wives came into the back-room, the Doghouse, and couples kissed beneath the mistletoe.

'How about it?'

'Hark at *his* cheek! *I* shouldn't.'

'I'm not asking *you*. I'm asking your *friend*.'

Jack Brough returned. He had a bottle of Scotch, still bonded, under his arm.

'Drunk am I?' he demanded as he walked to the bar. 'I'll give you bleeding drunk!' For a moment he was struggling to break the seal, and then the top was free. He lifted the bottle to his lips and swallowed. His raised head made prominent his Adam's apple and, as though it were an extension of his throat, the bottle was run through with bubbles at each swallow. 'E'll never do it.' 'He bloody will.' 'Lay you a quid on it.' 'Done!'

With a sudden wasteful splutter Brough lost the penultimate mouthful, spraying it across the sawdust and the crowd. He shook his head, eyed the bottle ruefully, and finished what was left at a gulp. 'He'll die, him.' 'Serve him right.'

He shook his head again. 'Now maybe tha can call us drunk,' he called triumphantly.

'Aye, Jack Brough, I reckon I can,' said the landlord.

They carried him back to his cheap green-walled bungalow. The door had been left open. 'Miracle he isn't dead, the daft bugger,' said the voice at his feet. 'Bigger miracle's him bringing the bottle all this way wi'out drinking it,' said the voice at his head.

The bungalow was one of a row, along an unmetalled road from the station. The road crossed the railway in front of the tunnel, along a narrow stone bridge. Brough's porch looked out over the railway and the valley floor.

'Looks as lights have just gone out at the Home.'

'What do the loonies do for Christmas, do you think?'

'Don't know. Best ask our Jack. He's biggest loony round here, I reckon.'

Brough responded vaguely to his name. He spoke thoughtlessly, accurately, 'It's all bloody evasion,' he said.

'What's he say?'

'Christ knows. Put him down. He'll be all right.' They lay him face first on the floor, and he swore at them for clumsy buggers. They left him, and the door open behind them.

'Happen fresh air'll do him good.'

He turned his cheek on the cold texture of the oil cloth. He felt its rubbered roughness, softened like a landscape under snow, against the tough bristles of his face. One eye at a time and the world seemed commendably normal, but with both of them at once it doubled and strayed. He looked out over Winfell, half hidden behind its cover of bare trees, wrapped in snow and darkness. 'I'm going to have that bleeder,' he cried. 'I'm going to burn the bleeding Home down one of these days, mark my words.' He screamed without making a sound.

David stood at the window of his ground-floor room, running his fingers around the sill. He could feel the holes where the mesh had been that had restrained Leonard; David was more trusted, and though his room was locked his window would open wide. It was a starless night. The rim of the valley was abrupt against a pallid snow-bearing sky. On the ground, in contrast, the snow was beleaguered: it had almost gone from the floor of the valley, although higher, beneath the millstone-grit edge, it still straddled the bracken.

Above David was a gutter, and it brimmed and dripped. He squinted up at it in annoyance. A train went along the cutting past the house, invisible, its pistons shushing the rattling coaches. He lit a cigarette: not all the patients were allowed to smoke in their rooms either. The confidential Christmas train continued towards Manchester; David saw its firebox glow, far away.

> The soil is sift and sodden flesh, the Soul
> Of England is corruption and decay.
> The bulbous roots that decorate the clay
> Make patterns like a head wound does, and roll
> Across his nose and cheek, a scarlet claw
> And talon of damp wood, a monkey's paw,
> Memento of the death within the bole.
>
> Scarlet worms with sharp round mouths that breed
> Between the grinning teeth left in the skull
> Tunnel the dull soil and trap the dull
> Nourishment of death, and as they feed
> They enter into contract with the roots,
> The patterning decay, the corrupt shoots,
> That suck the soil, the Soul, the sullen seed.

It was past midnight, and thus already Christmas Day, when he climbed into his bed. He tried to find comfort in his childhood, in memories of their ample Edwardian Christmases, and of nights of anticipation and bare restraint, but comfort eluded him and he was left only with sadness. When he dreamt, his dreams were shot with death.

The doctor woke first, with the warm smoothness of his wife beside him and the cold air making an island of their bed. He reached across and his hand came to rest on her thigh. The material of her nightdress was soft and enticing, and his hand lingered over each fold as it gathered it up.

Gently, without quite waking her, he raised the hem of the nightdress. His fingers, blind puppies, sniffed out the dark. Where the weight of her breasts pressed her body there was a secret fold. He traced its curve with his knuckle. She did not stir. Delicately he raised the fingers of his hand in turn, and let them buff her nipple.

'What are you doing?' she asked.

Guilty hands recoiled. 'Are you awake?'

She moved rapidly to wakefulness. She felt the tug of her nightdress hugged about her waist, and understood him.

'You made me jump,' she told him, as though apologising for her earlier surprise; he was all action now.

'Merry Christmas,' he said. 'We'd better get moving now,' he added, forcing a change in their mood. 'We've a lot to do today.'

She looked up at him as he sat in the bed. 'Merry Christmas.' She raised her arms. 'Don't I get a Christmas kiss?'

'Naturally.' He kissed her firmly, possessively. 'But we really must get up and about now.'

The patients queued for their sinks. In their hands were sealed safety razors. The orderlies watched them carefully, and felt uncomfortably authoritarian as they did so. They need not have worried. These public school and college men had washed communally all their lives.

David reached the sink. Because it was Christmas Day, there was an ironic piece of holly pushed behind the mirror. David washed seriously and thoroughly, as Nanny Rourke had taught, and patted himself dry with a towel. He dampened the badger hairs of his shaving brush. It was a fine brush, with an ivory handle double-banded in silver. He used it to whip up a lather in his shaving mug and then, watching himself in the mirror, disguised himself as Father Christmas.

The locked razor folded strips of foam as it passed across his face. He rinsed it beneath a tap, and matted dark bristles washed free. He brought the razor to his face again and continued to shave. He did not feel the cut, but when he washed the razor again, blood had made the foam pink and had darkened the cutting edge of the blade.

An orderly gave him a piece of coarse tissue paper. The orderlies always watched carefully when the patients shaved, because some of them reacted strongly to the sight of blood, but David seemed calm enough.

They returned to their rooms. David's room was downstairs. They travelled in slow, gaudy lines, in their silk dressing-gowns and with their white towels folded over their arms, processing slowly, half courtier, half waiter. They dressed in their rooms.

They had been instructed to dress carefully, as it was Christmas: David wore a black suit and a white, stiff-collared shirt, and a pair of elegant spats. The spats were brand new, and were his Christmas present from his mother; in return he had given her a garnet brooch. Dressed and ready, David waited for the knock on the door and the call telling him to go to the dining-room.

The dining-room was in the old house, across the passage from the annexe. The patients were pleased to see that the doctor and Mrs Penn had joined them for their meal. It was a good breakfast too, with kedgeree and kidneys, fried eggs and bacon. There was a feeling of lazy contentment about the table after they had eaten, which was increased when the doctor handed round a box of excellent Virginia cigarettes. 'A sort of Christmas present,' he explained. The air softened behind their smoke; the doctor rose to his feet.

'I think the first thing I must say,' he told them, 'is a big thank you on behalf of us all to Mrs Taylor and the rest of the kitchen staff for providing us with an especially fine breakfast this morning. And I've heard that there will also be an equally splendid lunch. I don't know about you, chaps' – the same unconscious British idiom, natural and therefore not at all embarrassing – 'but I think it would be nice if we could show our appreciation of Mrs Taylor's sterling work by washing all the crockery so that she can get back to her family this afternoon. What do you think? Do I have volunteers enough to help me do Mrs Taylor's tasks this Christmas Day?'

Hands went up around the table, fitfully, until the decision became unanimous. It was an unusual idea, but an amusing one. Sometimes at country houses David had found himself organised in preparing and serving meals for the staff, on the housekeeper's birthday or the day before a footman's wedding, and he had always rather enjoyed it.

The doctor continued, 'Secondly, something else I think is rather pleasant. The new vicar, Dr Morrison, who incidentally was attached to the Sherwood Foresters, has invited us to church for morning prayers. I'm afraid I don't really think all of you will be up to it, but I'd be glad to take a few of you. It'll be nice to join the congregation.'

There was a bit of a commotion. It was an interesting change in the routine, a trip to church, and the patients were fascinated. One or two were being rather silly about it, thought Mary: she hated to see these well-dressed men expose themselves as mad.

Not that they were all well dressed, she decided, as her eyes fell on George. George was across the table from her, not directly across thank goodness, but at a slight angle so that you didn't have to watch him eat. His table manners were revolting; his tie was beneath his ear. Indeed, all of George's clothes seemed somehow displaced. His collar was at a curious angle because he had mis-buttoned his shirt. His pockets bulged with unknown wonders and empty cigarette cartons. Drops of gravy and egg yolk patterned his shirt, and his nose ran constantly. Thank the Lord Clive won't invite *him* to church.

'Mrs Penn?' said George.

'Yes, George,' said Mary. She was unfailingly polite to the patients. They adored her.

'Mrs Penn? You will let me go to the church? I do so like to go, and I've not been able to. Not since my recent problems, you understand.'

Before Mary could reply her husband had spoken. 'Of course you can, George.'

George beamed in gratitude, and a dew drop stretched from his nose.

Mary turned to her husband. 'Can I have a word with you?' she asked in a low voice.

The doctor was being genial, chatting with the two patients on his right. 'Certainly, my dear.'

'In private.'

'Oh?'

He made an excuse and left, exchanging jovial greetings with those he had to pass to get out. Mary followed and said nothing. Her mouth was held firm and sucked in at the end of her lips. They left the dining-room and closed the door behind them.

'Well?' asked the doctor.

'How can you be so stupid?' said Mary. 'You can't possibly take George to church and you know it. Now the poor man's going to have to be disappointed, all because you can't say no.'

'What do you mean? Why can't George go?'

'I surely don't have to explain the reasons.'

'I'd like to hear them,' he said. 'He's well behaved.'

'But just think what he looks like! I can imagine them now, in the church, nudging one another and pointing at him. I'm afraid he just can't go, Clive. It wouldn't be fair on Dr Morrison.'

'Morrison wouldn't mind. He's not that sort of chap.'

'I didn't say he'd mind. I said it wouldn't be fair. It's all right for you, and for Morrison too, to have enlightened ideas about how to treat the patients. But as far as the rest of Grindlow, the rest of the world, is concerned, this place is an asylum. The 'ome, they call us. They don't like us. They put up with us because we keep ourselves to ourselves, but don't think you can go parading George around the streets because you can't.'

'Morrison said I could bring anyone I wanted,' said Penn, rather plaintively.

'Morrison's new here. He's a stranger. He doesn't know how the people feel. Why should he? He was in the war, he must have seen shell-shock before. In his job he'll have been more help to some casualties than the doctors. But if he's going to fit in here, in Grindlow, he's going to have to accept what Grindlow thinks about things. Not what was normal on the Western Front, or what is fashionable in Vienna or London, but what people feel in Derbyshire.'

'I see. You've been thinking about this a lot, have you?'

'Of course I have. You're not English, you don't recognise the subtlety of the way the English look at things. Nobody ever admits to bad thoughts in England. Nobody is going to tell *you* that all your patients should be shot for cowardice or locked up and the key thrown away, because you would condemn them for such thoughts. So what we do, we English, is find someone who agrees that the patients should be shot, and who thinks it a good thing that they should be locked away for ever in a darkened cell or what-have-you. It's what I said. Nobody in England admits to having bad thoughts: they just find someone who can convert bad into good with them.'

'What can I tell George?' he said, defeated. 'You saw how pleased he was when I said he could go. And he really is a lovely chap.' He thought for a moment. 'Perhaps I should telephone Morrison, find out what he thinks.'

'No!' She surprised them both by tenderly stroking his sleeve. 'Morrison would tell you to bring George along, which is the Christian thing to do, but that doesn't necessarily make it the best thing to do under the circumstances. You poor innocent, Clive. Don't you understand how people react to the thought of the clinically insane? You really must understand. Our patients are dangerous lunatics to the outside world. Take the nice-looking ones, the well-dressed ordinary ones. Make a good impression on the village. Take Gordon Keeman-Hardy and Alex Little and . . . some others.' She wasn't sure why she didn't say David Goodchild's name: she had intended to and then stopped. 'Take them. But don't take anyone the village can point to or talk about. Please!'

'All right,' he said. But what, he wondered, do I tell George?

They did not often administer drugs forcibly at Winfell. The doctor did not believe in policies of coercion; his way was to coax out the cure. There were, however, occasions when chemical restraints were necessary.

Two orderlies held George by the arms and pinned him to the bed. A third pulled down his trousers. His belt gave easily, for George had not troubled to fasten it correctly, and his trousers and underpants wrapped themselves messily about his knees. His pale legs became a waterfall that tumbled into the white foam of his underwear.

Penn squeezed the syringe experimentally. A tiny spurt of liquid was released, and the level of the syringe was corrected. He knelt on the crowded bed, between the body that threshed and the bodies that steadied, and rested his hand flat on George's buttock to keep him still. Being careful to keep the needle point well away from his own flesh, he pushed it into George, who screamed. Slowly, seductively, the doctor injected the patient. George continued to fight for a few seconds, and then the jerks subsided to wriggles and nothing.

They straightened up his trousers and left him on the high bed. Their eyes did not meet as they walked out of the room. It was all for George's own good, they reminded themselves, but it still felt like a rape.

Christmas bells appealed across the valley. The prosperous travelled to church by motor car, the rest travelled on foot. The patients of Winfell travelled by charabanc, 'The New Twenty Horse-Power Fifteen Seater Albion', recently purchased by the doctor for these outings.

The church at Grindlow was large and mainly Victorian in architectural style, although its origins were Saxon and it still boasted a Norman arch in the doorway, virtually hidden by the Gothic porch. It was too large for the parish it served on ordinary occasions, but on Christmas Day the farmers and shepherds came down from the neighbouring peak and it was full to the point of being crowded. Because of this influx the patients were not as conspicuous as Mary had feared, for which she was grateful; indeed, she thought they were managing very well, as they climbed down from the charabanc and along the damp stone paths to the porch, braving the gauntlet of the churchwardens.

The congregation sang its hymns of praise and gratitude. The doctor, though Episcopalian, was unaccustomed to church services and followed his wife in the complicated rites of kneeeling, sitting and standing, or in the sorting out of prayers and songs from innumerable small books. Dr Morrison led them confidently: he referred to the gallantry shown by the villagers of Winfell in the recent war, and even went so far as to offer a prayer for the patients of Winfell, wishing them a speedy recovery.

Dr Penn and the patients did not go to the rail to receive communion. This was another condition attached to their attendance by Mary, and a sensible one in the doctor's eventual judgment, as it kept them from the public eye. Not that there had been any problems so far: this small, selected group of six were perfectly presentable. Can't be too careful though, they had, after discussion, agreed.

Mary went to the rail alone, therefore, feeling self-conscious as all irregular communicants do. She knelt on the red carpet before the altar and tried to think of a prayer. God was a stern headmaster, Christ a talented but naïve young pupil-teacher; except for this morning of course, when Christ ceased to be anything except a baby in a manger. A server worked his way along the kneeling communicants. 'The Body of Our Lord Jesus Christ ... eat this in remembrance ...' The wafer was dry and soft, and broke on her palate. The vicar followed. 'Drink this in remembrance that Christ's blood was shed for thee ...' The wine was rich and sweet. She could not associate the drinking of blood with the baby in the manger. She offered another moment's blank contemplation in place of a prayer, stood, backed, bowed and returned to her pew. The new window, the Remembrance window, caught the damp light of the morning. 'Drink this in remembrance that Christ's blood was shed for thee.' She knelt down next to her husband, made the motions of another prayer, and then sat.

After the service Dr Morrison stood in the porch and shook hands with his parishioners as they left. There was a fine drizzle in the sky now, and the beleagured sun made a rainbow. 'I'm so glad you could come,' he said, offering a firm handshake. 'So glad you could come.' The congregation raised their umbrellas. 'Merry Christmas.' There was a dash through the gravestones to cars and houses. 'Merry Christmas.'

The sun canopy of the charabanc was quite inadequate against the rain. The patients and the doctor rode in the back, while Mary was with the driver. A successful trip, thought Penn.

They stopped outside the house, where the drive broadened before the steps, and climbed down.

'Look,' said Mary. 'Mistletoe.'

It grew in the branches of an oak that overhung the

drive. The branches dripped grainy dirty water on to them. The white berries were a sort of pearl.

'Clive? Are you going to give me a kiss?'

He complied gallantly. David waited. 'May I?' he asked of them both.

'Of course.' He kissed her gently on the lips. Their mouths pursed and parted. Another patient found the courage to ask and then a third.

They went in, passing through the house to the annexe. It was nearly lunch. 'How is everything?' asked Penn.

'Fine,' said the orderlies. 'Very quiet.'

The smoke in the common-room had thickened, despite an open window. The patients seemed happy enough and safe enough. He left them and went to George's room. George was still asleep. He looked no more dishevelled than usual. The doctor studied him for a moment, took his pulse and laid a hand on his forehead, and then left. Although George's drugged sleep was very deep, the doctor was gentle when he closed the door, to avoid making any noise.

Lunch was excellent. Partly because of the continuing shortage of food, and partly because he was an American, Penn had decided on turkey. An enterprising local farmer had started to breed the birds. The meat was dry and rather flavourless, perhaps, but the texture was good. He wished he could have offered wine with the meal. Afterwards they had cigars and sang 'I Saw Three Ships' before clearing the table and washing-up themselves.

David stood by the sink, his arms deep in the soapy water. He had a sieve in his hands. When he pulled it beneath the water it made a circle of finer bubbles beneath the coarse foam. He thought a little about the doctor and his wife. I do like them, he thought. He was content.

In the last week of December, in the pendent lull between Christmas and the New Year, the doctor suspended analysis. The patients had time to sit and smoke all day, if they so chose. David was trusted with pen and paper, and unsupervised in his room, they let him write several poems.

> I've watched the moon mount sable sky
> And thought of you and poetry.
> I've watched the snow leave winter trees
> And written this, intent to please.

He wondered about showing them to Mary, but pride would not let him: the verse was rather poor.

He read through what he had written, dozens of drafts and sketches.

> I'm sure I sign my love in several ways
> In copperplate across my restless thoughts

he frowned, picked up the next sheet.

> I'm sure I sign my love in several ways
> In copperplate for all to see, for though
> I try to hide my love, my love doth glow
> As the copper-edge of cloud the sun betrays.

He held the paper to the flame from his cigarette lighter. He first tried to burn the whole wad, some fifteen or sixteen sheets, but the ineffectual flame licked distastefully at the corners and refused to hold, so he held an individual sheet and set fire to that. He let it burn till the flames scorched his fingers and he was forced to drop it. It landed on the rug beside his bed, and after he had trodden it out he found it had left an indelible mark. He felt guilty and opened the window to clear the air. If they knew about this they would probably take his lighter away, he realised. He scrubbed at the mark. He could not tell if it were burn or ash; whatever it was it would not go. He tried to pick up what was left of his poem, but it had cracked and now it crumbled into dust.

There was another party to celebrate New Year's Eve, another subdued and pleasant one. They entered 1921 eagerly. It seemed a hopeful, incredibly modern year. It seemed a long way from the war.

CHAPTER FIVE

21 January 1921

Dear Mother,
Thank you for yesterday's letter. There's really no need for you to apologise for not writing as often as I do, as I'm sure I have a lot more time to write. On the subject of time, by the way, I have decided – belatedly, I'll admit – on my resolutions for the coming year. These can be briefly summarised as shorter naps and longer poems: the former is really to give me more time for the latter. I've been reading my recent poems – I have been writing a lot of rubbish, haven't I? To be fair to myself I've not really had the strength to work harder at my poetry, but now I really am feeling so much better I think it time to embark on something ambitious. After all,

> Fair seed-time had my soul, and I grew up
> Fostered alike by beauty and by fear.

I feel it is time I tried to convert that into a big poem, although, to judge from the books Mary Penn has been lending me, modern poetry has little patience with beauty, while I expect we've all had far too much of fear. I'm not sure whether I've the temperament to be a Modern really – my sensibilities are still Georgian I suppose – but I enjoyed enormously a line I read in an otherwise incomprehensible poem from Mrs Penn's library about not being Prince Hamlet but just being an attendant lord who is there to swell the crowd. We all feel like that these days, I think.

I must stop writing now – it is a nice day and Dr Penn suggested we should go for a walk up the hillside. Things really are very well organised here. I haven't seen the valley from above; I'm told it is very beautiful.

I will write again before the week is out.

Your loving son,
DAVID.

Despite the railway and the insignificant ugliness of the recent diamond-tiled bungalows of Grindlow and the Worsleys the valley was indeed beautiful. The doctor led them out of the drive and on to the quiet purposeless lane that draped like a noose over their part of the valley, meandering down from Grindlow, crossing the river, passing the nestling low hill farms, and eventually coming back to meet itself just beyond the Winfell gates. The patients walked along the lane until they came to a stile that led them north, and then they passed into the woods.

The woods at the floor of the Winfell valley, the doctor told them, are typical of the natural woodland of the area. Much of north Derbyshire has been replanted, he said, but here we can still see the Sissile oak, the birch and the rowan. They passed between the arthritic branches that scratched the cold air. Already there was enough bud unfolding improbably from the dead winter trees to cast a faint green hue, so that from a distance they were wrapped in a haze of green. Bilberries trailed along the ground, promising small pink flowers in the spring, and their mean tart fruit beyond that. Wood sorrel hid, almost dead amongst the grasses, its trefoil leaves folded and decayed for winter, and coloured as red as the stalk. Dead bracken made elaborate, heraldic patterns beneath the trunks at the wood's margin.

They climbed over another stile and left the enclosed woods. They were in a field that had recently held cows, and one orderly, jumping from the stile, landed in a cowpat. The other laughed loudly, and delighted in calling attention to the stained shoe. 'What a stink. You're not coming near me, not with that stink,' he said.

The field sloped increasingly, and a well-defined path zig-zagged from the ridges to the next stile. The doctor led them up. They crossed into the next field, grazed by sheep.

Climbing steeply they were soon able to look down on the valley. Many of the patients were out of breath. The doctor, caught between enthusiasm for the scenery and his sense of duty, called for a rest.

From where they were they could look out in three directions. The line of the valley stretched west to the foothills of the Pennines. In the clarity of the day they could see Mam Ida in the distance, and the dark humps of Kinder beyond. To their left as they sat, smoking and resting, was the pretty neat Worsley valley, hollowed by the amber waters of Lund Sitch. To the east, the river Derwent ran through Grindlow and south to the Trent. Above them still was the craggy frown of Grindlow Edge.

The doctor stood up, led off. They climbed higher, skirting the remains of an old quarry. Millstones, shaped but never transported away, lay tumbled on the quarry floor like tossed lost coins. They continued up.

They passed the main road to Sheffield. It curved north just beyond where they stood, and an omnibus, a single decker, trundled round the line that divided moorland from farm. They waved when it reached them and went past.

They crossed the road and continued north. David rubbed his hands in the cold. He was smiling.

'Come on, David,' Rupert cries.

'I'm coming,' I say, and I puff on up the hill.

We're walking over the Wrekin today. It's wet and misty, and the landscape seems covered, for some unfathomable reason, with orange peel. We're not the first to have been this way, which is rather disappointing but not, I suppose, surprising. Fifteen years ago the vogue was to go around in boats on the Thames, following Harris, George, J. and Montmorency the dog; now it's Housman's turn to be the fashion. There's something ironic about us following Housman's trail about Shropshire, of course. Rupert and I have left Oxford for the vacation, to pursue Housman and the idyll of rusticity; only last year Housman became Professor of Latin at Cambridge. Such is the way of the world.

'What are you waiting for?' calls Rupert, interrupting my thoughts.

'Sorry, just thinking.'

'Don't. It'll ruin your complexion.'

I climb the hill towards him. Rupert is a mystery to me, really. He sits around with his pipe and books, looking like a young gargoyle with ambitions towards impersonating Augustus John, but he's twice as strong as I am. I only agreed on this trip because I thought it would be easy.

He's ahead of me again, spurting away while I climb at what I consider to be my usual measured pace. 'Much Wenlock,' he calls as he sees the view, and then, as I knew he would, he starts quoting.

> On Wenlock Edge the wood's in trouble;
> His forest fleece the Wrekin heaves;
> The gale, it plies the saplings double,
> And thick in Severn snow the leaves.

Breathless, I improvise a reply.

> On Wrekin, here, your friend's in trouble;
> His legs are sore, his breathing heaves
> A gale to blow all saplings double;
> He struggles on while Rupert leaves.

Rupert looks at me blankly. 'That's not Housman,' he says.

I do not reply to this. Can he really be so stupid? I fear he can: he went to Repton, I believe. 'Shall we go down?' I ask, with commendable moderation.

Much Wenlock is a pleasant place. We sit in the inn and sup cheerful cider, growing increasingly cheerful ourselves if truth be told. I begin to notice the pretty maid serving. I decide that I shall engage her in conversation, make her love me, and then leave, breaking her tender rural heart. I stroll over to where she stands at the barrels.

'Hello,' she says.

I thought I was to initiate this conversation. 'Hello,' I reply.

'Have you seen this?' She holds up a copy of *A Shropshire Lad*. 'You can buy it here if you like.'

'Really?' I say. What does she think I'm doing here? Of course I've seen *A Shropshire Lad*, I nearly say: there's a copy in my haversack this minute, and another in Rupert's. But I don't say anything. I return to my creaking seat.

'Hello, Lothario,' says Rupert. 'What did she say?'

'She tried to sell me a copy of *A Shropshire Lad*,' I reply, grumpily.

Rupert starts to laugh at this. I am annoyed, and then not annoyed. I start to laugh too. We have another cider, and continue to laugh, and then leave for Much Wenlock station. As we go we broadcast parts of *A Shropshire Lad*, and try to sell our copies at inflated prices, but we don't get any takers.

'Let's get a move on,' said the doctor. 'I'd like to get to the top before dusk.'

'It's cold,' said an orderly.

'And dark already,' said the other.

'But we've hardly got anywhere yet,' protested the doctor.

The orderlies turned to look at the patients, standing cold and huddled, breathing noisily.

The doctor sighed. 'All right. We'll go back. But we'll go back a different route.'

'Yes, sir.'

They returned along Lund Sitch, dropping down its steep valley and following a footpath through Nether Wortley. This took them close by the railway line: they watched the crimson through-train from Manchester as it passed them, and coughed in the smoke that it left behind. Wiry fires withered the grass in the cutting after the train had gone.

They reached Winfell as the sun set. 'We could have got to the top and back easily,' said the doctor. No one replied. They went round the house to the annexe, passing dustbins that still smouldered with ash. Mary's birdbath stood in the wasteland between the buildings like a column in the ruins. The double doors at the end of the annexe led to the corridor by David's room. They pulled their boots across the shoe-scraper and then took them off, lighting cigarettes and blowing on their hands, before walking in stockinged feet towards the common-room. David put his boots into his room as he was passing. He was tired but happy, and scoured by the clawing branches in the breath-flecked winter air.

16 February 1921

Dear Clive,
A bit of advance warning before you get your formal invite. The Institute has been trying to

arrange a series of talks on psychiatry, that being all the vogue in London at pres., and like the true friend I am, I suggested your work at Winfell might make a decent subject for a talk. The committee agreed so, if you're willing too, we'll be hearing from Dr Clive Penn on the subject of the Treatment of Shell-Shock, or whatever, in the not too distant future. Probably early July, actually, which is fairly distant but gives you time to sort out your notes.

Drop me a line and tell me if you'll do it. And don't forget you can always stay with me when you come down to the metrop.

Give my regards to Mary.

All the best,
ALEX.

'Of course you'll say yes,' said Mary. 'You've often said you'd like to talk about what you're doing to a wider group. The Institute is exactly right. I'll tell father. He'll go and I'm sure so will his friends. This is just what you need. Perhaps too we could get some sort of funds: you know you've always complained that we can only afford the rich. I think it's a perfect opportunity. You must write to Alex to thank him, and I'll write to father and let him know about this. I ought to write anyway. I haven't been in touch since before Christmas.'

'Why don't you go down and stay with them?' asked the doctor. If I'm to be pressured into doing my duty against my will I don't see why you shouldn't be too. 'Your mother would love to see you.'

'All right,' she replied. 'I will.'

1 March 1921

Dear David,
I hope you got my card and present. As I write today it is of course your birthday: I do hope everything is all right for you. You certainly sound happier. How is the long poem? You haven't mentioned it for a while.

This is just a note to wish you happy birthday again and to show that I was thinking about you. There is plenty of gossip round here but no real news – I don't suppose the gossip *ought* to be written down, in case it is slanderous, or is it libellous?

Write back soon.

With all my love,
MOTHER.

3 March 1921

Dear Mother,
Thank you for the present, and also thank you for the note you sent actually on my birthday: it arrived first thing yesterday morning, and was lovely because it made my birthday seem to stretch into another day. Mrs Penn asked if I'm called David because I was born on St David's day, which is a good question. I see her most weeks, once or twice, and we talk about poems. She is a very nice lady.

The answers to your questions are, respectively, 'short' and 'libellous', but I don't suppose you can remember the questions now, so that won't help you.

Have you read this fellow Hopkins? Mary has lent me Bridge's edition, and it is very strange. Mary says Hopkins's poetry is very modern, and while I don't see how it can be having been written half a century ago, I have to admit that it doesn't seem to have much to do with Tennyson or Browning, or even Georgian poetry. The sonnets are the best thing, very powerful although shapeless. I don't think this man Hopkins could have read much poetry – he certainly doesn't know much about rhythm, although some of his poems still sound quite good when read aloud despite this.

I'm still having problems with being a Modern, if the truth be told. Mrs Penn would certainly like me to be one, but I don't think I'm very good at it. I'd much much rather be Keats. Still, if Gerard Manley Hopkins can be a Modern even though he wrote fifty years ago, perhaps I can be a Romantic and write now.

At least I'm writing again.

> Your loving son,
> DAVID.

> 18 March 1921

Dear Mary,
I'm so glad you are to come to visit us. Of course your father will go to Clive's lecture at the Institute. Wire what train you'll take and I'll meet you at the station. Have you seen the new Charlie Chaplin film? It's called *The Kid* and it is terribly funny.

Your father sends his love, and we both hope Clive is well.

> With fond love,
> MOTHER.

Mary breakfasted on the train: a cup of tea in Derby; sausage, bacon and grilled tomatoes by Leicester; toast and marmalade before Market Harborough. She enjoyed eating on the train. She enjoyed the sense that she was using time to the full. It seemed modern, and rather splendid.

London was signalled by a spreading of tracks, gas holders, houses. They tunnelled and cut to St Pancras. The span and the spread of the shed swallowed them up into a mystical world of smoke and bright posters. She climbed from the train and enjoyed the apple-fresh tang of 1921 in the clinking coke of the engines. She breathed it in, swelling her lungs with her knowledge of now, and walked confidently to greet her mother.

Mrs Cotterham waited at the open square that was the end of the platform, where daylight could not reach. They kissed formally and walked towards their taxi: Mary was thin and fashionable, her mother fat and fashionable; together they looked like the well-dressed archetypes in a *Punch* cartoon.

'We'll go to your father's first,' said Mrs Cotterham.

'How is he?'

'Looking forward to leaving London. There'll be no one left in the centre soon. Bloomsbury is overrun by the university already, and Harley Street and Wimpole Street aren't what they were. I think everyone'll be in the suburbs soon. Of course, you can't blame people, wanting to get away from the smog and the noise, but I've always lived in London.'

'Surrey isn't so far away.'

'It's far enough. Derbyshire isn't far away either, but we only see you once in a blue moon.'

'There's no comparison,' said Mary.

There was a taxi waiting for them: they climbed in and a porter loaded their cases. 'Thank you very much,' said Mrs Cotterham, slipping the porter a handful of change. 'Harley Street,' she said to the driver.

They pulled out into the Euston Road, joining a long line of waiting vehicles. The air was shimmering with exhaust fumes; Mary could not see a single horse.

London's marvellous, she thought: it's so up-to-date. They passed the noble arch outside Euston station, and the elegant modern offices that lined the street.

'You'll like the new house in Surbiton,' her mother was saying. 'And your father loves it. It backs on to a golf course.'

'Hello, Father,' said Mary. He stood and let her kiss him.

'Hello, Mary. How are you? How's your American?'

'We're both very well, thank you. How are you?'

'Keeping busy.' Dr Cotterham smiled. 'You've heard about the new house? Have you seen the plans? Has mother told you it backs on to a golf course?'

'I can't wait,' said Mary. 'It sounds lovely.'

'You'd like it,' he said. 'Ever so modern. I've often thought that's why you married Clive, you know; because he seemed so modern. What could be more up to date than a psychiatrist, except perhaps an American psychiatrist? Still, a lot of good that did you, eh? Ending up in the back of beyond like you have. I never thought you'd leave London.'

'Neither did I,' admitted Mary, laughing loyally at her father's comments, but not knowing whether her loyalty was to him or to her husband. 'Still, I don't suppose we'll always be in Winfell.'

'I don't know,' warned Dr Cotterham. 'Your Clive seems very fond of the place.'

They had dinner in the town house. 'I'll miss this house,' said Mrs Cotterham to her daughter.

'No you won't,' said Mary. 'It's cold and inconvenient.'

'I will,' insisted Mrs Cotterham. 'It's all right for you. You're still young enough to be able to keep up with fashion. I can't. You can learn to drive and have your hair cut short and wear short dresses and make your bust disappear. I can't. I'd like to live in a stable way, that's all, where nothing changes.'

'Mother,' mocked Mary. 'You'd like to live in a stable, like an old pony, that's what it is. But me, I'm a racing car. I want to be modern. I like 1921.'

'I know, darling,' said her mother, sadly. 'You sound just like your papa. But honestly, Mary, it would break my heart to smoke a cigarette in public.'

The next day they went shopping. Mary had her hair cut and bought a new dress. Her mother made no comment but thought both hair and dress too short. Mary knew she would.

'I'm twenty-nine, Mother. I hardly managed to be young before, because of the war. Let me have a last few years before I settle into matronhood.'

'What will Clive say?' asked Mrs Cotterham.

'Clive?' asked Mary. 'I don't suppose he'll notice. But perhaps someone will.'

In the afternoon Mrs Cotterham returned, alone, to her house. Mary continued to walk through the busy modern streets. Sharp colours enticed her from hoardings and shops. Motor-cars played syncopated melodies. And once, overhead, magnificently, an aeroplane was a Cubist bird in the sky.

She walked through the West End. At Hyde Park Corner a man on a crate lectured on the follies of capitalism, and a good-natured audience jeered. She passed through the crowd, through Belgrave Square and Sloane Square, and found herself on the King's Road. The streets were rich with brightly dressed girls and men in soft collared shirts. Mary pictured the men as all painters, and her mind made bohemian garrets where the soft-collared men erected their easels and the brightly dressed girls undressed. Mary suddenly found herself wanting to be a brightly dressed girl on her way to undress, to lie on a couch in a picturesque room, to have an artist's sharp eye study her body. It was a thrilling, wonderful thought. She saw the attic, the skylight with the cracked pane, the artist with his palette and his charm. He looked at her carefully, checking her proportions against the thick pale-brown brush he held upright in his hand. His face, she learnt with a start and a blush, was David's.

23 March 1921

Dear Mother,
How are you today? I'm sorry I didn't write yesterday, but I barely had time to think. The doctor took us out again, just into the garden, and showed us all manner of living things which, to be honest, I should never have seen had I been on my own. And then in the afternoon Mrs Penn actually called to see me in my room, which she has never done before. She's had her hair cut, and looks terribly modern, like one of those women you see in the drawings in the newspaper, advertising clothes shops, but not so tall. She bought me a present in London, a volume of poetry by a man called Ezra Pound whom I once met before the war. He's an American, and very odd. So is his poetry. I've been reading it constantly. I don't understand much of it, I must admit, and I'm not sure what I understand is actually very good poetry. But I rather liked this bit:

> The age demanded an image
> Of its accelerated grimace,
> Something for the modern stage,
> Not, at any rate, an Attic grace.

I keep trying to write modern poems but they come out wrong, I feel. If it wasn't for Mary Penn I don't think I'd bother. But she does keep trying to influence me, and I must admit to being flattered by her interest, and so I persevere.

I'm getting stronger all the time. The doctor sees me nearly every day and we talk. Sometimes we talk about the past, other times we discuss my dreams. I don't always agree with what he finds to say about me, but it is good just to talk about myself to someone who listens and tries to help. I've even written a short poem about the war, which I haven't done for ages. I think this proves how much stronger I am. I was reminded of this by a silly incident which happened here yesterday, and wrote the poem then all in one go while I was meant to be reading *Hugh Selwyn Mauberley*: one of the sheets blew from the line outside the house, and flew down the garden. It was really exciting to watch!

> The washing, drying in the sun,
>   Flutters, folds and flaps.
> It's strung out from a heavy gun
>   As if it were perhaps
> Some fixed and gentle ammunition
>
> For pillow fights and harmless wars
>   Where no one ever dies.
> There's peace in our domestic chores:
>   We dream – our washing dries –
> Of pillow fights and harmless wars
>
>   Where no one ever dies.

It is funny. I hadn't realised this was a sad poem until just now, copying it out for you.

    I mustn't overtire myself. I think I will stop writing now.

              Your loving son,
                        DAVID.

CHAPTER SIX

THEIR CROWDED EASTER train pulled out. The windows were open, the cushions were hot. The sleepy, smoky air, like a child with dirty hands, made smuts on all their clothes. They left Sheffield behind, and their thoughts took on the rhythm of the train: the Whitby excursion, travelling north, trundles through towns with improbable names; past linear streets, grimy pit-heads, a cartwheel and lattice of steel and blue sky; beautiful towers, churches with spires, in-between houses built of cheap brick. The railway, like some extravagant metaphor, united everywhere. Ganglia and nerves of steel. A symbol of modern times, with the chattering telegraph lines accompanying it like musical staves.

They passed over rivers and canals, through early fields of barley, and corn that was green still but hopeful. They came to York. Before and after the station they could see three towers for the minster and snatches of white city walls; in the station the whole world became railway. Then they carried on, across the Plain of York and through the North York Moors, where the train wound its way through a beautiful wilderness of valleys. They craned out at the windows in wonder, and the marvellous train carried on.

First it was the smell. The Whitby air had a taste to it, salty, feline, feminine. It made them light-headed and hungry.

Then there were the masts, rearing up against the quayside. They felt they might race to those masts like children, but managed to walk in a dignified way. Finally it was the sky, blue with white birds that were bent and bowed like the foam at the crest of a wave.

They looked over the quay at the boats. The estuary water was greasy and jelly-fish stained. An anarchy of masts and ropes resolved itself into the squat integrity of the hulls below. They watched as the men in heavy boots made the jumbled ropes significant, and then, moving away from the side one by one, as ice breaks, they pushed out into the flow. The boats left diesel trails of blue smoke, and the water was writhed with dull and colourful oil.

As the boats pulled out, the doctor led his party away. David found himself urged on, though he wanted to watch as the boats raised their sails in the bay, and to follow the flocking mocking sea-birds. He found himself by Mary.

'You must keep with us,' she said. 'We don't want to lose you.'

'Isn't it grand,' said David.

'It's lovely,' she agreed. 'We come here every year, you know. Have you ever been here before?'

'No. I suppose everyone else has?'

'I suppose so. It doesn't change, although the weather is better this year.'

'The weather's lovely.' David grinned. 'Everything is.'

They waited by the swing bridge. It was twelve years old, and barnacles had gathered on its fat, cogged legs. The cogs revolved noisily, grating tooth into tooth. Slowly, smartly, astonishingly smoothly in contrast to the grimacing, tooth-grinding noise, the flat back road surface rejoined with a silver seam. A man in navy blue opened the gates at either end, and the swarming gawping trippers trooped across. Steel-workers from Middlesbrough, weavers from Leeds, occasional raw-voiced Scots. They pushed together and filled the narrow lanes. Their raucous womenfolk travelled apart, in merry groups, while the men, sombre in black and with serious faces, pondered about where to drink. The doctor threaded his party over the rutted cobbles and rotting fish. They sifted through the shifting crowd. It was hard to keep his group together, he found. They passed fishmongers, where the fresh smell of the sea mingled with sweet decay, and saw through the legs chalked prices, buckets of shellfish, slabsided cod on the slabs. They reached a long flight of stone steps. Here too the Easter people jammed and chattered. 'It were as good a cup of tea as any,' they were informed. 'Tha'll not get up them steps.' 'Have you quite finished, dear?'

They climbed away from the harbour scrupulously, counting the steps and avoiding the people climbing back down. 'Ninety-four, ninety-five, ninety-six, ninety-seven, ninety-eight, ninety-nine, one hundred.' They reached the top, disputed the number, and took a rest at the head of the steps. A man with a barrow sold tea, tuppence a white enamel mug, but the queue was long and the day was hot. The doctor led his patients away from the steps, into the graveyard of the fine Georgian-and-older church at the cliff top, and checked that the group was complete. To his relief, it was.

It was peaceful, in the graveyard, looking down on the town and the steps. The voices from below were muffled. They sat at the edge of the mown grass, facing the harbour and the sea. From here the houses were red-ridged tiles, fissured by hotch-potch streets; the fishing boats were still in sight, apparently stationary while the quick stripes and furrows of the waves went beneath them. In the distance the currents were patterns in the sea, like the oil in the harbour water.

They sat between old tombstones. It was easy to see from there how the harbour water differed in texture from the sea. The sea was playful, was puckered and pocked with shadowed dimples; the harbour, contained within two stretching moles, had the flat sheen of domesticated water, of ponds or mill pools. The doctor lit a cigarette and inhaled the view. The ancient tombstones ringed them. He yawned. He loathed the long train journey, the crowds and the rush, but it was all worthwhile to be here, now and on a day like this.

He let the patients recover their breath. They always seemed to enjoy Whitby too, but he knew that his own reasons for being there were selfish. He liked to look at the sea. Perhaps everyone does, he wondered.

He looked around at his patients, at his wife. There she is, laughing with David Goodchild. Her head rocks gracefully back and forth and her fine pale neck is stretched. David is laughing too. He's a strange one, thought the doctor. He seems so sensible, so ordinary and sane, but he's remote too. Were he to engage life more closely, life would destroy him, decided the doctor. And David recognises that.

The cigarette burnt down. The doctor stood up and ground it into the grass. In previous years he had taken the party into the church at this stage, to marvel at the hierarchic Hanoverian interior with its competing, jostling box-pews trying to get nearer to God, but last year the parish had put up a plaque in memory of those who had died in the war. The patients had enough reminders of war without that, felt the doctor. He led them towards the abbey.

It was but a short walk. The abbey was built high above the town and the rivermouth, and its plateau had turned into a meadow. Behind it was a green pond, spiked with weeds. They walked in a group round the ruin, extending their circuit to take in the pond, and saw the abbey reflected in the cold waters, with the blue sky and white clouds.

When they had been right round they sat down on the grass. The doctor did not want his patients to go too close: the abbey was poorly maintained, and despite the warning signs several people were climbing the ruins, dislodging rocks as they searched for gulls' eggs or strove to impress their girls. 'Serve 'em right if they fell,' said an orderly.

The doctor looked round at his patients. They looked quite dapper, quite respectable. Some of them looked almost relaxed. Then his eyes fell on the comic figure of George. The doctor wanted to smile, but he thought then of Christmas and could not. He made a decision: I'm going to do something for George.

He turned back to admire the ruins, their stubborn grandeur, their determination. Cromwell had been a farsighted man, thought Penn, to pepper England with these picturesque remains. Clive Penn's education, naturally unconcerned with the niceties of English history, did not distinguish between Thomas and Oliver Cromwell. He lit another cigarette. He had, despite this, learnt a lot about England in his eleven years in the country. He found it fascinating and beautiful. An Anglophile east coast American, from an Anglophile family that had christened him Clive, his cultural standards hardly seemed alien at all here. Clive: a quaint, colonising, un-American name. He blew a smoke ring, puckering it between his lips. England has merely given me a taste for the genuine. He thought of his wife.

He had met her at her father's house. At a party just before the war. She was eighteen, and blushingly pretty; he was thirty-one, a bachelor still and aware of it, and an American abroad. Fortunately for him, she was reading Henry James at the time. They were attracted to one another at once.

Then the war had begun. The doctor had just completed his studies, and had been appointed to a teaching post in London. He never took up the post, but volunteered immediately for war service. Because he was a doctor, and because he could not ride, he was made a trooper in the lancers. Letters, via his professor and his friends, eventually found him a commission and a job as an army surgeon, and from then on until his wound and his MC – he was shot while dressing a casualty in no-man's-land – he served on the Western Front.

He lay on his back and the sky was blue and clear. The few clouds fluffed and puffed pompously and ineffectually; the sun was a familiar friend. He thought back on his war. It is not difficult to be a doctor in the war, he decided. The job after all remains much the same: to save, not to kill. For the others – he thought about his patients – it isn't so easy. They have to learn to kill.

Perhaps it was this that led me to specialise in shell-shock? The sea-birds, though white, were dark against the sky. They flew overhead on slender strong wings. Penn dozed and thought of Mary.

I smiled at the man in dressy black, but that makes him even more suspicious. What is he? A vicar? A church-warden? A verger? An ageing curate? I'm Episcopalian myself, but I can hardly make sense of these Anglican clerics. Whoever he is, he seems hostile towards me. I guess I should have worn my uniform: he's thinking I'm a shirker.

Where's Mary? If she doesn't turn up soon I'll be thrown out of this place. I hadn't expected Westminster Abbey to be so fraught. Nor so empty: there's just me and this verger guy. And he's walking away, thank God. This reminds me – I walk to a wooden chair, one of hundreds ranked and filed in the aisles.

'Our Father which art in Heaven,' I murmur as I drop on to the crimson hassock, 'Hallowed be thy name. Thy Kingdom come, thy Will be done.' Another voice joins mine. 'In earth as it is in Heaven. Give us this day our daily bread.'

'Mary!'

'Sssh. I'm praying. And forgive us our trespasses, as we forgive them that trespass against us . . . For thine is the Kingdom, the Power and the Glory, for ever and ever. Amen.

'I remember Miss Marchbank taking us through that prayer,' she continues, pulling herself up from her knees and sitting on the chair. 'You probably won't have noticed, but when written out, by Miss Marchbank at any rate, the Lord's Prayer is just the same shape as the British Isles.'

'No, I hadn't.' She looks so adorable in a small white hat with a veil that I want to take her hand at once. Sense prevails. She might say no.

'I suppose it's because God is English,' she says.

'I always thought he was Jewish.'

'You mustn't say that here. The walls will tumble down, like Jericho.' I suppose she's joking, but how do I tell. I know so few English women.

'Are you going to show me round?' I ask.

'Certainly. This is the Abbey. That' – she points – 'is the roof. This' – she leans across me prettily and touches – 'is a pillar.'

'Thank you, ma'am,' I say, as we would say at school. I can be sarcastic too, I guess, but I have other games to play. 'Myself,' I add, continuing with the role of dumb Yank, 'I could get to kinda like this place.'

'I'm being silly,' she says. I think it is an apology. 'I'll show you what I like here.' She leads me up the nave. We pass the verger again. He looks more disapproving than ever. Beneath the tower, where the kings of England are crowned, we turn right.

We reach a place of statues and plaques, less organised than most. 'Poets' Corner,' she tells me in an awed voice. 'This is where I shall be buried.'

'Really? I didn't know you were a poet.' I'm probing for advantage now.

'Oh yes. Quite a famous one.'

'You must show me your poems.,'

She smiles and turns back to the dead. I find it difficult to be interested. My eyes travel upwards, as they are meant to in this place, and follow the vaults as they pattern the roof. A door leads off to the chapter house and I step through it. The chapter house is surprisingly airy, and seems to swell from a single, stylised, tree of stone. Which perhaps it is. I wish I knew more about these things.

Mary steps through the door beside me. 'Are you interested in poets?'

I turn to make a flippant or charming answer, but see that it was a question asked in real seriousness. She is intelligent enough to deserve my truth, for what that is worth. 'No,' I reply. 'I'm not really interested in anyone who is dead. I see enough of death. I'm only interested in the living.' Not perfectly expressed, I'll admit – I've no pretensions to be a poet, living or dead – but she understands and nods sensibly.

'Shall we go to the Henry VII chapel?' she asks, quietly. She is a very special young lady.

The Henry VII chapel turns out to be rather special too. I had not expected such a change from the rest. The ceiling first attracts the eye. It is astonishing, frankly, and I must have gasped or something because I can hear Mary laughing at me. I look at her with as much mock-severity as I can muster, but it is a friendly laugh that does not seek to ridicule. I laugh right back and look around once more. The vaults conspire in the middle, like stalactites, or like the fruits of ever more fanciful stone trees. Between the branches the shadows are deep and dark, so the ceiling seems somehow crisp and well defined. I'm beginning to wish I were a poet, so that I might describe this better. In the middle lies the dead king, and his wife. I know next to nothing about Henry VII. I know that he really was the father of Henry VIII – in America this can confuse: we tend to think that all the English kings must come in batches, like the first Georges. I look at this statue. For the father of Henry VIII, Henry VII seems a thin man. I remark on this to Mary.

'It's true,' she says. 'You know, I've often thought that perhaps Henry VIII grew into his name. It's that "Eight" of course. All those "I"s make it ever so fat.'

'I suppose so,' I say, uncertainly. I'm not actually clear what she's talking about. Sometimes, as now, she seems almost childish, and somehow that is part of her charm.

'What sort of man was Henry VII?' I ask. 'I see him as vain and proud to have built all this splendour, but the man in the statue looks wise and pious. It doesn't seem to fit.' This is true. The tomb seems to belong to a different age. The splendid vaulting is so Gothic, so involved and organic; the figures on the tomb are languid and realistic, with little lions like dogs at their feet. The architect of these vaults could not have made such tame lions, and neither could the sculptor of those elegant hands design that crowded pendular roof. Between the two, however, I lose all sense of Henry.

We leave the chapel and walk to the foot of the tower. Banners hang from the walls of the nave.

'You're not wearing your uniform,' realises Mary.

'I know.' Ours is not the kind of war you wave banners.

'What are you thinking?'

'Nothing.' I try to change the subject. 'What are you doing for lunch?'

'Nothing.' Is she parodying me?

'Savoy suit you?' I ask, taking my courage in both hands and presenting it to her.

'I would be charmed, kind sir.'

This is better. This is what I came on leave for: for the unreality of love. 'The pleasure will be all mine,' I say.

'No,' she says, and she is being serious again. 'Not all yours.'

This change of mood affects me: my mind goes blank yet I speak none the less. 'Mary,' I say, and it is not clear to me whether I am responding to her sudden seriousness or to the playfulness of the moment before. 'I love you.' I had not intended to say this. The words slipped out so easily but now I find they seem to block the air between us. They fill the cathedral like a shout.

'Why, Dr Penn,' she says. 'This is so sudden.'

I look at her. For a moment what she has said does not register and I think that she is returning to the level of play-acting. At least that gives me an opportunity to save face, to laugh my declaration off. Instead of doing that though, I plunge on. 'I shouldn't have said that.'

'Why not? Isn't it true?'

'No. Yes. Of course it's true.' I'm losing track; I'm losing everything. 'It wasn't fair to say it.'

Now she is certainly smiling, laughing at me even. All along she has been laughing at me, I realise, but I have been too blind, too egotistical, too optimistic, to see that till now. In my head I review her actions and words since we met, and each one seems calculated to mock.

'Why ever not?' she asks.

I want to leave her now. I do not want to beg, or be a figure of fun any more. I want to leave her now, but I can't. And because I have nothing else to say I revert to my old line. 'It wasn't fair to say what I just said when I might be killed in the war.' My old excuse: it held up well enough when I thought she might care for me; now, faced with her barely disguised contempt, it sounds so flabby and forced.

'I'll take that risk,' she says.

I don't understand.

'Stop standing there with your mouth open,' she tells me. 'You look like a goldfish. Do you want me to marry you or not?'

'Yes,' I manage to say. 'Yes, I do.'

'I thought so. Why didn't you say so?'

Eternal hope bubbles in my breast. 'Will you marry me?' I ask. I ought to have dropped to one knee. It's too late now but I wish I had.

'Yes. Oh yes.'

We were a step apart; now we are clinging. I kiss her once, on the lips, through the knots and nets of her veil. She splutters and throws the veil back and we kiss again. Over her shoulder I see the verger, watching us in disgusted horror. Our lips part and I smile at him. He turns smartly away.

I do not care. I have grown to fill these vaults. Ducking to miss the hundred foot roof, I lead my fiancée out to the sun. I did not hear the choir come in, but now I hear them singing.

The doctor jerked awake suddenly. His cigarette had burnt out; the sun was behind a small cloud. He looked around, re-establishing himself in the present, and while he was still lost in time, he saw the ruin of Whitby abbey. The pointed arches, holding up no roof, standing proud of the once-proud walls, seemed the melancholy failure of all his dreams. He saw a future when Westminster would look like that. Briskly he stood up, and out of temper led his party away.

'Hold on a moment, Clive,' called Mary. 'We haven't all finished eating.'

'Sorry,' he said shortly. 'I thought you had.' He looked back at the abbey as he waited. The sun had passed its zenith now, and the shadows reached east for the sea. A herd of cattle ambled through the loose masonry by the pond, and drank long healthy draughts.

They walked down the hill, down the steps, and re-entered the push and the squabble. David still walked with Mary: they talked animatedly of Pound and Hopkins, and touched together as they passed through the crowd.

The doctor was wondering what to do for George. A word with Morrison might be an idea.

George ran his greasy fingers across his waistcoat and sang silently 'For those in peril on the sea', opening his mouth appropriately but making no sound.

They passed the lifeboat station and a bandstand. They were on the quay opposite the abbey now, where the road sloped up to the incongruously named Khyber Pass. The uniformed bandsmen played 'Oh We Do Like To Be Beside The Seaside', and sweated a lot. Nearer, a Punch and Judy show cynically ritualised marriage and the law; they watched for a while, behind rows of children on low wooden school-room benches, as sausages and gallows were raised, battered and lowered in glorious misanthropy. The children loved it, and so did the patients; Mary and the orderlies thought it silly and were glad to move on.

They climbed from the quay to the North Cliff, up modern paved steps cut into the grass, and between the geometry of the bedding plants.

'It's curious,' remarked David, 'how these seaside paths, whichever resort you're in, always have suspicious patches of dampness on the steps.'

'I know,' agreed Mary. 'Where do you think they come from?'

'Better not ask, I should say.'

They reached the top. The abbey was silhouetted across the harbour; this side was modern and commercial. Large white hotels, distinguished from their neighbours by the name and the colour of curtains, swept a crescent round a display of Works Department flowers: pansies and early chrysanthemums littered the grass with colour. They promenaded along the front, while the docile sea lapped the shore sixty feet or more below. The crowd here was less than in the old town that nestled below the abbey, and was better dressed. The patients were required to raise their hats to the women they passed: couples walked with parasols; nannies pushed prams. They looked over the edge at the sea. A crowded margin of sand held off the waves, reinforced by children wielding buckets and by bathing-huts. Adults, on hired deck-chairs, sat beneath gathered handkerchiefs and ate their sandy-wiches. Half-way down the steep slope of the North Cliff, where the funicular railway tottered beneath the grass, was the great red-brick edifice of the Spa Pavilion.

'It was neither up nor down,' hummed David as they descended to the pavilion. Externally it looked like a railway station; internally it was like a rather old theatre, in need of redecoration. The doctor had booked their seats in advance.

The matinée show was always of the best quality on Easter Saturday. It was old-fashioned but slick. A juggler juggled; a fat man sat comically at his loved one's feet and sang to her; a young man rode a one-wheeled cycle and the orchestra played Sullivan's favourites. The sterile Easter Saturday audience loved it. An elegant lady reappeared at the end – she had sung a song of high romance earlier in the programme – and made a short speech to the accompaniment of a deep drum roll.

'Ladies and gentlemen. And now, to close, a delightful old song that I know you all know, written by my dear friend Ivor Novello. Ladies and gentlemen, a song that will live for ever. Please feel free to join in, so long as you sing in key!'

The band struck up; the doctor winced. The woman filled her lungs and sang:

> They were summoned from the hillside,
> They were called in from the glen,
> And the country found them ready
> At the stirring call for men.
> Let no tears add to their hardship
> As the soldiers pass along,
> And though your heart is breaking
> Make it sing this cheerful song:
>
> Keep the home fires burning
> While your hearts are yearning,
> Though the lads are far away
> They dream of home.

'Mummy. Why's that man crying?'

> There's a silver lining
> Through the dark cloud shining

'Bolsheviks. Ought to be ashamed of themselves. Walking out on Naomi Clarke like that.'

> Turn the dark cloud inside out
> Till the boys come home.

The hysteria was complete. Each one of the patients had broken down. The song came to an end, perhaps a little abruptly; in a muttered silence the doctor led them out. The daylight when they reached it was bitter on their tear-washed eyes. Mary hung on to David's sleeve with one hand, comforted another patient simultaneously. 'It'll be all right,' she told them. 'Come on, back to the train.'

They could not really hear her, or see the seaside town. Their ears filled up with gunfire, their eyes with the sniped and blood-drained trenches. They moved through a sloping half-dark in the brilliant afternoon sun.

They could not board the train until five. Company regulations. Mary, the doctor, and the orderlies, walked the patients round and round.

Exhausted, they travelled back. Penn sat by George, who misfastened and unfastened the buttons of his jacket constantly. Mary sat opposite, with David next to her. David slept.

'A long day,' commented the doctor.

Mary smiled back her agreement. 'It was going so well.'

'It's best to be philosophic about these things,' he said. 'After all, they were enjoying themselves until then.'

'Aren't people stupid.'

'It's not their fault. They didn't know the patients would

be in the audience. It's a pretty popular song, after all, even now.'

'Not them, silly.' They talked in low voices. 'The ones in the audience. "I was in the war too," said one idiotic man when I tried to explain. "I was in the war too."'

'It isn't worth worrying about.'

The doctor looked out of the window. It was growing dark. The gas jets above their seats were lit by a guard with an electric lighter. The world outside turned monochrome, turned cinema, turned off; the windows looked back on themselves, and reflected chiaroscuro heads. The doctor saw himself, and the empty moon beyond.

The window had misted at its corners. On the opposite side of the train an orderly made patterns on the glass. The train passed through a station and the condensation lit through, leaving the darker space the finger had traced. 'This way home,' it said. Penn liked that. George too was now asleep. Penn half stood, pulled down the blind, and shut out the moon and their faces. David woke gently and looked up.

'This way home,' the doctor said.

CHAPTER SEVEN

WHEN A HARPIST plays her harp her face is grave, serene and wise; the sun that day had such a face, and the valley was warm and lovely.

A fox felt his way through the feline bracken. He placed first one delicious paw and then the next on the dead undergrowth; his head and tail were long, low, and held in lissom tensions. Slinking, sliding, sliding forward; smoothly gliding; gently, gently.

Then calamity of feathers, catastrophe of squawks. One bird got away. The fox crushed its tiny speckled eggs. A spittle of yolk wet his whiskers. He licked up the eggs and their shells, and broke the other skylark's neck. He took the broken bird in his jaws, and leapt and ducked through the bracken away.

The survivor hovered above the scene, scolding irresolutely. But it was a skylark, and on the wing: gradually it climbed the dulcet air, and its sweet song rose with it.

David was in the garden, as were all the patients. He pushed his Dutch hoe through the soil and listened to the skylark's song. He looked up, but could not see the bird through the perfect liquid sky. 'Thou art unseen, but yet I hear thy shrill delight.' The patients near him took no notice. They were used to irrelevant comments, non sequiturs.

The heat of the sun took the tension from his muscles

and his mind. 'Such harmonious madness,' he muttered. He rested with his arm around the hoe and looked round. A butterfly tangled with a flower's head, sorted itself out, and drank delicately. David took his cigarette case from his shirt's breast pocket, while his arm was still entwined about the hoe. He flipped the case open, selected a cigarette one handed, tapped the tip twice on the silver lid. It was a marvellous day.

The doctor sat in the surgery, although he expected no consultations that day. He made notes for the lecture he was to give to the Institute, while the tempting sun tapped at his window. 'The Treatment of Shell-Shock. By Dr C. L. Penn, MC, MD.' he wrote at the top of the page. He looked for a ruler but could not find one, so he used Mary's sharp steel paperknife instead. The blade tapered to a point, and his nib, following it, left a line that trailed off beneath his name. 'God damn.' He started to write.

Mary looked out of the window. Idyllic, she told herself, seeing the patients working in the garden. She decided to take a stroll.

She looked in on her husband before leaving. 'I'm off for a walk, dear,' she said.

'I envy you,' said the doctor.

'Care to come?' asked Mary.

'I can't. I've all this work to get through.' He yawned and stretched. 'My lecture for the Institute. I hope they appreciate it.'

'You shouldn't have left it so late. You've had since February to write it.'

'I've been busy.'

'Well, don't expect sympathy from me, that's all.' She left him and went outside. The day was very warm. She heard the sound of bees and of hedges being clipped, and saw the patients working.

I see our work at Winfell as two-pronged, wrote the

doctor. *We aim to take the pressure from our patients, to give them the opportunity to discover for themselves the particular stimuli which induce the symptoms of their neurosis, fugue or neuralgic shock. And at the same time we try to occupy them in tasks that are useful and constructive and that will, in measure, replace the weight of their memories and memory-induced psychosis with new, dis-associated, responsibilities. In the winter the men are encouraged to paint, sew and knit – I hope to include facilities for pottery and perhaps even weaving in the coming years – whereas in the summer the attractive grounds of Winfell occupy much of the patients' time and energies.*

David wore a straw hat. He looked absurd to Mary but rather wonderful, like some Romantic hero who should be travelling with his donkey. David waved to her happily when he saw her. 'Hello,' he called. Many of the other patients also waved. Mary was very popular with them then. She walked down a strip of lawn between two herbaceous borders, organised between mellow brick walls in approved Gertrude Jeckyll manner, and greeted the patients as she passed. David, in his outrageous Robert Louis Stevenson hat, smiled broadly at her. His face was shadowed, his teeth white.

'Could I speak with you?' he asked.

'Of course.' She stepped to one side to hear him as, in a low voice, he thanked her for the help she had given him in Whitby. 'It was nothing,' she said. 'You were just tired. Everyone was tired.'

It is our conscious policy, wrote her husband, *to avoid reference either by word or deed to the patients' psychoses or psychoneuroses.*

'I'd have been stuck without you.'

Our aim is to be as unobtrusive, and as helpful, as is possible.

'I'm dreadfully sorry about what happened.'

'There's no need.'

'Was I really awful?'

'You were very tired,' she repeated, patiently.

He looked at her gratefully and she smiled at him. 'Shall we go for a walk?' he inquired unexpectedly.

She looked quizzical. 'A walk?' she asked.

'It's a beautiful, wonderful day,' he said, by way of explanation.

Many of our patients are barely neurotic. As Professor Freud has so admirably revealed, the distinction between normal and abnormal, clinically speaking, is far less than we have previously supposed. If we, for the time being, isolate childhood, again following Professor Freud's example, we find this curious fact ... The psychotic or psychoneurotic conditions suffered by my patients are no worse than the normal psychopathologies of everyday life, with one important addendum: my patients' experiences of adult life are exclusively experiences of war.

'All right,' said Mary. 'Why not?'

He laid his hoe down on the grass and offered her his arm; she accepted it gracefully, resting her hand on the careful crook of his elbow. 'Where to, my lady?' he asked.

'Just one moment, sir,' she said. 'I can't take you off like this. You're meant to be working.'

'"Cela est bien dit, mais il faut cultiver notre jardin."'

She laughed with him. 'Precisely. Frank!' she called. 'Frank Leighton!' One of the orderlies turned in their direction. 'Frank. I'm taking Mr Goodchild here for a walk. I don't want you to think he's run off.'

'Right you are, missus.'

Winfell is not an asylum; officially it is called a 'sanatorium' which, given the public school background shared by all our patients, is a familiar and, we hope, none too forbidding word.

They walked along the red gravel drive and out through the gates, turning left along the lane.

Incidentally, it is an unfortunate economic fact that it is really only those of public school background, the officers rather than the other ranks, who can afford to take advantage of the facilities of Winfell.

The road arched beneath a cathedral of elms and oaks, and the stained-glass leaves cooled and refracted the sun.

They reached the railway bridge. The road ducked underneath the track, and within that single dark arch it was almost cold.

'Brrrr,' said David, covering Mary's hand with his own. 'Let's run.' So they did, laughing through the sunlight and up the slope at the far side. A train tooted cheerily in the distance. 'Shall we wait for it?' asked David.

'Let's,' said Mary.

He offered her a cigarette.

'I shouldn't,' she said, taking one. He sheltered the flame of his lighter against the faintest of breezes. It was a balmy day. In the cup of his hand the flame was orange and hard. He lit her cigarette and took one for himself.

She looked at him conspiratorially. 'I'm still not sure whether ladies should smoke,' she said. 'In public, at any rate. What do you think?'

He took his hand from the flame as he lit his own cigarette. Out of the shadow the flame disappeared, for all the world was flame. 'I think it's splendid.' At this moment, thought David, everything is splendid.

The train whistled as it approached. It steamed merrily through the sun, puffing out white smoke and grey smoke, making the sky-striping telegraph lines vibrate. It shone with polished brass and crimson; it was punched with white highlights of sun. It went past, and they waved, and the people in the train waved back. Then it was gone, leaving a low dying mist of acrid coal smoke that lingered between the nettles. They walked on.

Suddenly a tandem swooped at them, whooped by, dipped beneath the railway bridge and disappeared. They were left with brief images of the couple: his moustaches, her billowing skirts, the sense of their freedom and delight.

'We must get one of those,' said David, impetuously.

Mary put out her cigarette. 'Come on,' she said. 'We'll go through the woods to the river.'

She ran ahead, but he caught her by the kissing gate. 'I won,' she called, slipping through the gate.

'Nonsense,' said David. The gate swung towards him as she reached the other side, and he was shut out. 'The best you can claim is a draw.'

'We'll see,' she said, running ahead of him again, leaving him to negotiate the gate. She ran along a wide path through the trees. The ground was studded with the occasional horseshoe mark; pale yellow flowers clustered beside the path. David ran behind her, running easily. Her dark hair, short and boyish, bobbed in Peter Pan waves as she ran, and her sportive dress ran too in the cream and pleated sun. He caught up with her.

'I'll put a girdle round the earth in forty minutes,' he claimed, running ahead.

He saw an oak. It stood, solidly in the centre of the path, splitting two earth tracks around its trunk. It had been climbed before, and often: the footholds nooked between its branches were worn smooth, and some philanthropist had helped the climb by adding strategic nails. David ran at the tree. The nails had rusted to the soft brown of acorns, and were cleaner on top where the feet rubbed. He gripped a wide branch and swung himself up, pushing up with his shoes on the nail. He lay down on the bough, recovering his breath, and Mary caught up with him, laughing at him and the race and the world.

He lolled his head back between forked branches. 'How now, spirit! Whither wander you?' he caled to the upside-down world.

'Bravo!' she replied.

He grinned at her, and twisted so he lay on his chest. His face was elfin through the oak leaves. He slipped an arm down towards her, touched her hair, fingered a single brown lock that the running had loosed.

'Or should I be Oberon?' he asked.

He stroked her soft hair as he spoke, and studied the leaves of the tree.

> I know a bank whereon the wild thyme blows,
> Where oxlips and the nodding violet grows
> Quite over-canopied with luscious woodbine,
> With sweet musk-roses, and with eglantine:
> There sleeps Titania some time of the night,
> Lulled in these flowers with dances and delight;
> And there the snake throws her enamelled skin,
> Weed wide enough to wrap a fairy in.

He dropped down beside her. His landing left him on one knee before her; he took her hand, pressed it to his lips, and held it in both of his.

'My prize,' he cried, joyously.

'For what, good sir?' she asked.

'I won the race.'

They continued through the wood, side by side now. There were bluebells lazing beneath the trees, misting the shadows. A woodpecker began its diesel tapping. A squirrel, crossing the path in front, continued to run vertically, impossibly, up the trunk of a tree. They looked at each other and around, and everything they saw seemed to ravish and bewitch.

They reached a clearing. A stretch of brown fur took fright at their approach and shot away.

'A rabbit,' said Mary.

'A hare,' said David. 'Though you don't usually see them in woods.'

'Perhaps he came for a walk, like us.'

She sat on the grass and arranged her skirt; he hitched up the crease of his trousers and knelt beside her.

'We should build a willow cabin here,' she decided.

'It would be awfully chilly in winter.'

'It wouldn't ever be winter, silly.'

She lay back on the grass and closed her eyes. The

sunlight was still red behind her lids. David picked a stalk of grass and chewed it, rustically, at her head.

'Isn't it marvellous here,' she said. 'It's so peaceful. You feel that nothing could disturb us. I do like that: we can't be disturbed, can't be reached by telephone, can't be contacted in any way.'

David thought silently for a moment before he spoke.

> I can't be reached by telephone:
> I'm resting by the meadow
> Where leaves leave dappled shadows
> And the trees trace gracious lines.

Mary laughed. 'What's that?' she asked.

'I don't know,' said David. 'I made it up just then, thinking about what you said. "Improvisation for an Idyll" by David Goodchild.'

'I'll give you another line if you like.'

'Thank you, Miss Inspiration.'

'What about "I can't be contacted by post"?' She turned to look at him, resting her hand on her arm.

> I can't be contacted by post:
> I'm dozing by the river
> Where the fat fish flash for ever
> And the coots and moorhens rest.

'We haven't reached the river yet,' pointed out Mary.

'Poetic licence. You can lie, so long as it makes sense.'

'What about another line. What about "I can't be traced by telegram"?'

> I can't be traced by telegram,
> I'm with a lovely lady.

There was a silence. 'Is that the whole verse?' she asked.

'What more could you want?' He threw his arms wide,

embracing the wood and the world. 'What more could anyone want?'

He stood up. 'To the river,' he said, giving her an arm so she could rise. Her flesh was unexpectedly cool; she felt him strong and careful.

It was not far. The river was placid and clear, with narrow rills and spouts between rocks, and tidy pools where water-boatmen scuttled. Amber stones lay precisely, emphasised beneath the water by shadow and shadowing moss. David found a flat stone on the bank and skimmed it over the water, but the river was not wide and the stone bounced straight across, clattering among the rocks on the far side. He turned back to Mary.

'Don't look,' she cautioned. She was sitting on the grassy bank, her skirt hitched up to her hips, unrolling her stockings. David did his best to obey.

She stepped into the water. It was cold and glorious, and the mossy round stones had the strange texture of peaches beneath her feet. She gathered her skirt in front of her, but the water got deep quickly, and the folds kept escaping from her hands. She caught her hem as it touched the water, and stepped out.

'Aren't you going to paddle?' she asked him.

'Why ever not?' He took his shoes and socks off, and rolled his trouser legs to just below his knee.

'The water is quite deep quite soon,' she warned. She was tucking her skirt into the mysteries of her underwear. For the first time that day David felt a little afraid. 'You must watch your balance,' she said. He stepped in. The water was cold: it surprised him and made him think of her flesh.

She waded in beside him, and then beyond him. Her legs were white and shapely. David watched her splash through the sun-flecked, foam-flocked water. She seemed suddenly terribly naked beneath her clothes. He looked down at his own legs. The water jumbled about his calves, and the hairs on his legs caught tiny bubbles that were pearls or other jewels.

Mary made her way through the water to him. The sun was hot and loving. He untied the string strap of his wide-brimmed straw-hat, took the hat off, put it on her head, and then his hands fell uselessly to his sides. His awareness of her had begun to hurt.

'Thank you, my chevalier,' she said. His hair was golden under the sun. She raised herself to kiss him, gently, on tip-toe. Suddenly she slipped. He caught her. She hung from him awkwardly. For a moment they clung together for protection, and then their balance was secure, but they did not part. Their lips touched and pressed. Her arms went around him. The sun-hat slipped off and fell, crown-downward into the stream. They let it wash away.

The doctor was still in his surgery. The cold northern light washed the white walls. *Above all*, he concluded, *it is our intention at Winfell to make our patients feel wanted. So much of the problem, for so many of them, is that they have been excluded from the routines of daily life for so long that re-adjustment is not possible. While they are outcasts their minds will naturally return, time and time again, to the thoughts at the root of their ostracisation: to the war and the horrors of war. If we are to return these men to society, restored to health and usefulness, we must recognise this: the greatest gift we can give them is not medication; it is not even our expertise and experience. Our greatest gift, ladies, gentlemen, colleagues, is love.*

CHAPTER EIGHT

Before he left for London Penn called in at the vicarage and spoke to Dr Morrison. The two men got on famously. Morrison agreed to the doctor's suggestion: they would begin, on an experimental basis, the next week. 'Not a word to anyone at Winfell though,' requested Penn. 'Let it be a surprise.'

The same time the following day saw him eating at a table for one in the dining-room of his London club. The evening sun through the Georgian windows cast a net of square shadows over the diners. Penn dipped and sipped at his soup; his cutlery, as clean and cold as the waiters, queued beside his plate.

The conversations around him were loud and intrusive, spoken in tones more accustomed to command than social intercourse. Words brayed at him across the genteel dining-room: 'Another bottle, eh?' 'Splendid show, old man.' The voices of the English ruling class, thought the doctor sardonically. He took refuge in his soup and his US nationality.

As the sun dropped lower and hid behind the buildings opposite, the waiters lit the old-fashioned gas lamps mounted on the walls, but these efforts were briefly outshone when an errant ray of the sun escaped and struck the chandelier. The room at once was crystalline, suffused with crimson light, and the moment became fixed with a mineral intensity. Then the sun passed behind the buildings once more and this brilliance was extinguished. Penn finished his soup. I mustn't worry about this evening, he told himself: I'll be all right.

Constable Mather dismounted. It was far too warm that evening to bicycle up Grindlow hill. One hand on the handlebars, the other on the saddle, the constable pushed his bike up the road.

David sat alone in his room. He finished a cigarette, stubbed it out, and reached for another. Ten to nine. One hour and fifty minutes left.

The room was pallid with smoke. He opened his window to clear the air. It was still quite light outside, although the sun was down. Bother this, he thought, returning to his book and pretending to read.

Anticipation settled uncomfortably in Mary's stomach and knees. This rather surprised her; she had not expected to be nervous. She pushed the plate away.

She went to her sitting-room, and found a cigarette in the box by the window. She lit it with the silver lighter that sat on the ledge. The wheel was stiff and grazed her thumb; the flame was weak but sufficient. She inhaled gratefully, and blew self-conscious puffs of smoke through her lips. She went to the chair and sat down.

By the chair was a book. It was an American book: Clive's brother had sent it with his last letter. 'This year's sensation. Everyone's read it. I'm afraid, brother dear, that it marks the end of your period of high fashion. Last decade we all loved the warriors, the men in uniform. Especially those in British uniform. But I guess that period's gone. Now it's the time of the men who went to Princeton, not Europe.' She picked the book up. *This Side of Paradise*: an attractive title, and the book started well, but she was in no mood for fiction. What was it David had once said? Fiction is life without the inconvenience of living? She put the book back down again.

There was a copy of *The Times* by Clive's chair, where he had left it that morning before going for his train. She looked up at the clock over the mantelpiece: twenty past nine. He will be starting his lecture soon.

She stood and went over to the window. Outside, the twilight dulled the valley like a dew. She returned to her chair.

The newspaper by Clive's chair annoyed her: so familiar, so faithful to her absent husband. It was opened at a page of classified advertisements, and she found 'Lectures' announced between 'Entertainments' and 'Picture Theatres'. She looked anxiously for her husband's name, but the only mention of a doctor was one Dr James Porter Mills of New York, and his lecture was on Spiritual Healing. Of all things, thought Mary.

Determinedly she leafed through the paper for distractions. She looked at the Harvey Nichols advertisement: Gowns 39/6-59/6; Morocco Handbag 29/6; Charming Wrapper (illustrated) in flowered Crêpe de Chine 49/6. Wouldn't it be nice.

Mr Shaw had a new play, *Blanco Posnet*, at the Queen's Theatre from Wednesday; various cricket matches were won or lost; Ireland continued to dominate the centre pages. She continued to turn the pages. Here was an advertisement for liver salts; there, a glamorous photograph of the contestants in the University Air Race.

Her eye caught a small piece, 'Nerve Specialist To Lecture'. She read it reluctantly: 'Dr Clive Penn, MC, MD, is to lecture on the treatment of soldiers subjected to nervous shock tonight at the London Institute of . . . ' She put down the paper and found another cigarette. Quarter to ten; only sixty minutes to go.

She picked up the American novel with sudden decision and crossed the corridor to her bedroom. The shutters were closed, although it was still not fully dark, and the lights were on. She sat on the bed first, and then wriggled over to lie there, and read the book carefully. The door, although resting against the frame, was deliberately not fastened.

Jack Brough watched the last stopping train of the night pull out. He pulled the envelope from his pocket and looked at it again. He was tempted to open it, but fought the temptation and won. I've not opened it yet, he told himself: and I've had the bleeder in there since lunch. It can wait a while longer. If it's what I think it is, I'll be getting drunk after I've read it any road; then I might as well get drunk first. Happen I'll not mind reading it so much if I'm drunk.

There were two full bottles in his office. He broke the bond on one of them and started to drink, carefully and seriously. The words of an old song came back to him.

> I don't want to be a soldier,
> I don't want to go to war.
> I'd rather stay at home,
> Around the streets to roam,
> And live off the earnings of a lady typist.

He laughed, took another mouthful, and sang out loud. Constable Mather, riding past, did not bother to record that he had heard Jack Brough singing when he went by the station. It was becoming increasingly regular, this drinking of Brough's.

It was time at last. David stood, straightened his tie in the mirror, and tiptoed out, his shoes held in his hands. The linoleum was uncomfortably cold to his stockinged feet, and the air domestic with snores. He crept carefully towards the passage that led to the house, his way lit by a rotund moon. The corridor seemed endless to him in his urgent fear: squares of floor-pattern, window-frame, concrete buttress and beam slotted into a Chinese box of perspective that was dashed by diamonds of moonlight. He reached the doors to the passage and slipped through, standing stock still as they closed themselves behind him. His mind focused on silence.

He walked through the passage quickly. The moon was overhead. From the scullery he could look out over Mary's bird-bath, chiselled firmly in the picture-house monochrome rubble. He made his way cautiously over the tiled floor, loosely covered with rugs, and then a rug slipped and he fell.

Ten, eleven, twelve, thirteen, he counted to himself. He lay still, anxious, braced against the sudden light which he knew would come. Improbable excuses rose like flotsam from the wreck of his hopes, and he clung to them desperately. Sleep-walking (though fully dressed); heard an intruder; don't know why my door wasn't locked, never happened before. His heart was beating everywhere: in his ears, his legs, his hands. He could hear it echoing around the room.

And nothing happened. He carried on.

He opened the door from the scullery to the hall and went up the stairs. The carpets here were warm and kind after the linoleum and terracotta. When the stair creaked his mind shocked him with the painful image of the butcher's hooks in the scullery roof. He waited again for discovery.

Mary's room was on the left. David, who had lived in the house for a month before moving to the annexe, had no trouble finding his way. He moved a short distance along, and then stopped to put on his shoes. There was something undignified about arriving barefoot.

Mary had been waiting for him alertly. She opened the bedroom door and put a finger to her lips; the yellow light from her electric lamp silhouetted her, and made a halo of the few stray hairs.

She stepped towards him, but instead of embracing him she took his hand. He saw she was fully dressed: a dumb disappointment numbed him. 'Upstairs,' she whispered. 'Not here.' He tried to kiss her but she shook her head and led him down the corridor. Behind them, Mary's door, ajar, still let slip its wedge of light.

'Should we turn it off?' whispered David.

'Doesn't matter,' she whispered back, but still she returned and flicked the stiff switch. They were both a little disturbed by the new darkness, and moved closer.

She took him to a door which opened to reveal a falling shaft of moonlight and a climbing flight of dusty wooden stairs. There were no carpets, and their feet made hollow slaps on the boards, but Mary did not seem to worry. The attic rooms were obviously deserted.

'Here,' she whispered, opening a door. The room they entered was also lit by a skylight, and the blind spying moon had followed them in. The room was sparsely furnished – the impersonal remains of a servant's room, after the servant had left – and the bed, wrapped in an iron bedstead, was single. Mary tightened her hand on his and then released it.

She stepped back and he followed her. He put his arms around her and kissed her. She let him, moulding her lips to his for a while, and then pushed her hands on his chest and moved back, further into the room. She smiled nervously.

Slowly she unbuttoned her blouse, standing before him, looking neither at him nor away, but through him and beyond him. He felt glorious discomfort rising. She slipped the blouse off and unfastened the skirt; it fell to the floor and she stepped from its ring. Once more he made to move towards her, but she stopped him with a wider smile.

She sat down on the bed. His lower lip tucked between his teeth, and he sucked and bit gently. The weight of her breasts jerked her brassière forward as she unclipped it, and the straps fell from her arms. Her breasts were smooth and white, and cupped and tipped with shadow.

She unfastened her stockings and rolled them into rimmed discs that she discarded, and then quickly, surprising him, she lifted herself slightly from the bed and rid herself of the last of her clothes. She put her arms out to him. He stepped forward, pulling off his clothes in a frenzy that was partly pain. She kissed his naked stomach and drew him to the bed.

Their lips met. Their tongues fished for secrets, and like fish they slipped and darted. Hands touched and explored. She felt the delicate bones of his spine, tracing them up in their ridged arc and spreading her hands across the shoulder blades; he rolled his fingers across the nipples' fine firmness or stroked up between her white thighs. Her hands joined him there in the darkness. Gently, persuasively, she drew him towards her moistness, and then he needed no persuasion and became a pain that grew easier and better, while his body made the awkward contractions of sex. His movements were urgent and unhappy. She lay beneath him with her eyes wide. He felt all his being squeezed to a tight point and then burst within her, and she watched the moon through a dirty pane.

Dr Penn sat down to applause and the chairman stood up to speak.

'I would like to say, on behalf of us all, how grateful I am for that informed, humane, and above all encouraging account of work at Winfell. I'm sure I am not alone in having had to rethink my views on chronic disability in the light of these fine words. And now, if Dr Penn is willing, I'm sure many of you will have questions you would like to ask.'

The chairman turned to Dr Penn, who nodded his assent.

Constable Derkins finished his tea, put his cup down and picked up his helmet.

'I'll not be back while eight,' he said as he fastened his bicycle clips. 'Get a decent night's sleep, love. You'll have to get used to me working nights.'

She smiled, tiredly. 'I miss you.'

'I know love.' He went to the door. 'And I miss you and all. Don't get up,' he told her. He went into the narrow hall and she heard the front door open and close.

He rode down the hill to the police house. Mather was waiting for him.

'Evening,' said Mather.

'Hello. Anything happening?'

'Nowt.' Mather started to push his bicycle homewards. 'Brough's a bit noisy down at station, but there's no trains due. Arthur Calow's heifer's got summat up with its innards. And I reckon Bill Wright's round Daisy Bakewell's place again, but there's nowt we can do about that one!'

Refusing to share his colleague's salacious pleasure, Derkins mounted his bicycle. 'Goodnight,' he called.

'Night,' replied Mather as he disappeared around a corner. 'Hope it stays fine for you!'

'I don' wan' 'o be a djoldier,' he sang, 'And lidge odge earnings odge ladgee ty-pissed.' He lay on his back on the platform bench and contemplated two moons. They made fat round eyes in the sky. He winked at them and one disappeared. God's winking back, he thought: perhaps he's pissed too.

Brough groped beneath the bench for a bottle, and in doing so rolled off. He found himself on his face among cast-off tickets, but continued to feel for the bottle without a pause. He found it and, sitting up, held it towards the sky. I'd offer you a drop but there's nowt left, he thought, shaking the bottle upside down in proof.

Has tha seen this trick? he wondered.

He raised himself unsteadily to his feet, picked up a second bottle, and held them both by their necks. Their hollow mouths faced him like the guns of a firing squad. One, two, three. He threw the right-hand bottle into the air, and shifted the left into his right hand. The flying bottle spun triumphantly and landed in his vacant left. Higher nex' time, he told God.

One-two-three. The bottle spun in the moonlight, glinted, and caught the guttering of the wooden station building before bouncing off and on to the rails. It smashed conclusively. He sat down on the bench. It's not so much of a trick wi' only one bottle, he thought, apologetically. He put the survivor down.

A sudden light played mysteriously at the far end of the platform. Brough eyed it with curiosity. Is that you, God, he wondered. Me an' God, we're like this, he thought, crossing his fingers at the light.

'Who's there?' asked a voice, and Brough became agnostic again. God wouldn't speak with a Derbyshire accent.

'Who's there?' replied Brough.

'Who's there?'

'Are you taking the piss?'

'Oh, it's you is it, Jack Brough?' The light resolved itself into a policeman with a lamp, who walked round the end of the platform and through a gate in the wooden palings that kept the public from the track. 'Drunk again?' asked the constable, walking along the track.

I hope a train comes, thought Brough, but he said nothing.

'I asked if you were drunk.' Brough still did not speak, though his lips moved. 'I heard that!' said Derkins.

Brough turned away. 'As if I care.'

'You'd better. I'm warning you.'

'What's tha going to do?'

'You'll see,' said Derkins, impotently.

'Fine.' Brough sat down on the bench. He felt depressed. He remembered the letter in his pocket, still unopened. The thought of it depressed him further. 'Are you standing there all night or what?' he asked.

Derkins, looking up from the track, neither spoke nor moved. Brough looked down at him. Bugger it. He fished in his pocket for the letter and drew it out, splitting the envelope with his thumb nail. 'Dear Mr Brough,' it began, and it ended, with clumsy irony, 'Your obedient servant'. 'Contrary to the policy ... ' he read. 'In direct contravention ... safety ... ' 'Bollocks!' The last word was cried out loud.

'You what?' asked the policeman, but Brough did not hear. His head was bowed in the moonlight, and his hands crumpled over the letter. Derkins watched for a while.

'I'll be saying goodnight, then,' he said.

Brough did not reply, but shook his head slowly from side to side and then dashed it into his hands. The screwed up letter seemed to froth from his hands like water or beer.

'I said I'll be saying goodnight,' said Derkins.

'Aye,' said Brough, looking up. 'I'll be saying the same, then.' The voice was expressionless. He had reopened a cut he had made shaving that morning, and a trickle of black blood ran cautiously down the line of his throat.

'I'll be off then,' said Derkins, hesitantly, and then he turned on the indecisive gravel between the tracks and walked away. Brough watched without seeing as the policeman let himself out through the paling gate, and sat lost in thought beneath the paling moon.

The military policeman hands over to a sergeant. 'In line. At the double, march!' I set off, bouncing my weight on the flagstone yard. 'Halt!' An officer takes over from the sergeant. 'Thank you, sergeant.' 'Thank *you*, sir.'

Four dirty walls and a dirty French sky. At one end of the court is the prisoners' post, and behind it the wall is cleaner where the bullets have chipped. I look at the low cloud. The rising sun cowers back there. What a day to have to die.

The padre reads. He's like everyone else in the bleeding army: commands and instructions; thou shalt not kill, thou shall not commit adultery, thou shall not sleep with thy neighbour's ass.

The clean white cloth around the eyes. Some more sententious rubbish from the padre. The last rites; what about the last wrongs I wonder, and the pun doesn't make me want to smile. 'We are but thy servants, Lord.' Then it's to the post – not tied to it, unexpectedly; it's just somewhere to lean. And then the lousy orders start again.

'Firing squad shun,' says the sergeant. 'Ready?' asks the officer, polite-like. 'Aim.' Rifles click: money going in a till. 'Fire!'

The sound echoes through the square, and then it is quiet again. Another order – the officer sends a doctor forward. 'See if that chap's dead, will you.' In the army you are not dead even, unless a superior tells you.

'Dead,' says the doctor, flatly. 'Mort.'

'Good show,' says the officer, but he says it quiet, like even he doesn't mean it. Looking at him closely now I can see him white at the top of his neck where his face fits. The sergeant takes over. 'Firing squad shun. A-bout turn. At the double, march!'

My mind hurts with resentment. 'We are but thy servants, Lord.' Tomorrow we go back to our regiments. We're all serving on different sectors. They prefer it if we don't talk about the executions. We're to carry out the orders and then shut up. When this war is over I'm never going to be told what to do. Ever. They've had their chance, our la-di-dah rulers with their posh noses and useless chins, they've told us what to do long enough. And, let's face it, a right bleeding mess they've made of it all too. Look at this, shooting our own bleeding side. Look at it all.

I sit on my bed. A bombardier from one of the heavy

regiments walks down the rows, and then a major. There's a crease on my blanket.

'There's a crease on your blanket,' warns the bombardier.

'Strip this man's bed,' yells the major. His face has turned scarlet.

With conspicuous gallantry the bombardier does that, heaving at it. A blanket farts in two. 'That's torn it,' whispers someone down the barrack room. 'Silence!' bellows the major.

The bombardier looks apologetically at the blankets. The major snorts. 'Serves the man right.' And then, to me: 'You made your bed, you'll have to lie on it.' He laughs a lot, unpleasantly, like a saw going through bone.

Jack Brough made his preparations slowly, as though he were avoiding committing himself: he did not think consciously about what he did, but carried on in an alcoholic certainty that made action better than inaction and noise better than silence.

The key to the lock-up hung from a nail on the left inner door of the office; concentrating on no more than that, he went to fetch it. He felt it hard and cold in his hand.

He walked along the track some fifty yards, until he came to where the lock-up stood away from the up-line signals. The moon gave a dull sheen to the rest of the world, through which the polished tracks incised. The moon made more shadows than the sun, and seemed to find the texture in all things: liquid iron rails; gnarled and grained sleepers; the shattered gravel aggregate. Ahead, in the distance, the windows of the signal box were warm and inhabited; they spoke longingly of sandwich boxes and mugs of tea.

Brough ignored the chance of company. The key slotted into the padlock and turned. There was a click, and then the lock dangled in front of him like something broken, swinging from its one bent arm. Inside it was dark, and he barked his shins. He did not swear. He picked two cans up from the floor by the door, held them up to the moon to read them and, satisfied, carried them off. The door he left ajar. It opened inward, so half of it was shadow, and half the sign on the door. 'Fin Store,' it said, and underneath, 'Anger.'

He went back along the track. The cans were heavy against his knees. He returned to the office and put them on the desk. They leaned unevenly on a sprawl of newspapers and timetables. He left them there and went outside, to sit once more on his bench. He still refused to admit he had made a decision.

An owl called sadly through the still night. The letter that had announced his inevitable dismissal was a ball of white at his feet. He picked the paper up and opened it, but screwed it back to a ball again without reading a word. He stood up, returned to the office, and picked up a can.

The paraffin spurted diffidently, like a cheeky child, on to the desk and chair. The can swallowed air and spat. To begin with he was nervous, and then he found the pleasure in the task. An intoxicating reek rose in the room. In the half dark of the office the gulping stream became a flow and then a trickle, before ending in shaken drops. He threw the can down and its tinny thump was hollow. He picked up the second, began to unscrew the top, and then paused.

His fingers tightened the cap again. He left the room and did not close the door. The can was familiar in his hand now. He walked back along the track, past the hut and the signals, and then ducked behind the hedge to avoid the bright signal box. The signalman was not visible – probably asleep, thought Brough – and the owl called out again.

When the track ducked into the shadow of a cutting Brough returned to it. The sleepers were firm under foot and he made better time that way. Not that there's any hurry, he thought, but there's nowt to gain by hanging about, either road.

He walked nearly a mile before climbing the bank. He pulled himself up on the sparse vegetation, and hurt his free hand grasping brambles. At the top was a gaunt strand of barbed-wire, held aloof of the drystone wall on wooden pickets. He had climbed the bank to the wire before, many times, in France, though the tall trees that blocked the tilted horizon gave his *déjà vu* a complicated and dejected quality.

He threw the can over the wire and into the trees. It clanged and glugged, and he thought it had burst, but after he had eased himself over the wire and recovered it he found it was sound. He lay down on the grass, clutching the can, waiting for the sound of bullets.

For the first time he was conscious of birds, singing in the telegraph wires and the trees. They brought him back from France, and made him realise that it was later than he had thought. He stood up. 'Come on, you daft bleeder,' he said. 'This time it's for you.'

Winfell was screened from the line by a double row of poplars, planted by the coal merchant who had built the house. They were almost mature now, thirty feet high, slender and elegant. Beneath them a tangle of hawthorn and self-setting birch gave way to low ground-covering plants, hosta and geranium. The fat leaves of the hosta cracked juicily under his feet, while the incongruous flowers stalked his passage.

Ahead of him there was the annexe, and beyond that the roof of the house. The moon had almost gone now, giving way to a gentle dawn that lit the sky to his left, over Grindlow Edge and Lund Sitch. Urged by the threat of the sun he hurried on, skirting the lawn and its rows of formal roses, and keeping to the herbaceous shadows.

A brief dash took him to the nearest corner of the annexe. His heart had started thumping chaotically. The fall of the land meant that even the ground floor windows here were well over his head; none the less, he doubled over as he passed beneath them. He moved carefully, where the house was skirted with gravel that shushed him indiscreetly as he walked.

At the far end of the annexe he saw an open window. He was surprised, and full of a righteousness of drink. Don't they even lock the maniacs in? Cautiously, feeling vulnerable and almost ridiculous, Brough stood on the can and, correcting its metallic wobble, was able to look in. There was enough light to show him a bedroom, and to show that it was empty. For a moment he wondered if the occupant was only out temporarily, but the bed had not been slept in. He stepped down from the can, which overbalanced and fell down, making guilty nervous noises in the gravel. He lifted the can to the sill and rested it there; awkwardly, grunting, he climbed in, snagging himself on the bar that stopped the window swinging free. He found himself crouched on a desk with a chair.

The room was surprisingly comfortable, more like a hotel than a hospital. It couldn't be a patient's room, thought Brough, and then: I'll bet it bleeding could.

Brough splashed the paraffin gloriously. Hatred comes of envy and fear. It no longer mattered if he were caught – perhaps it had never mattered. The bed was soaked with paraffin now, and he turned to the carpet and chair. He lit a match and dropped it on the bed. Ready? Aim. Fire!

The flame surged, coming from all the surface of the bed at once and escaping hungrily through the window. He felt it pass over his head and linger in his hair. Panicking now, he climbed on the desk. The chair was already caught up in obsessive flame. He fell through the window with his clothes on fire, and in a rush of fresh air the clothes burnt brighter. Beating his chest to keep the fire from his face, he crushed through the brash gravel and ran across the lawn.

'Oi! You! Stop!' A light came on. He saw it cast a pattern of dangerous light on the grass beside him, and turned away from it. 'Oi! Stop!'

Brough could not stop. He stumbled towards the shadows. The flames died back from his clothes, leaving frayed ends that knotted and glowed. 'Oi!' cried the voice, and then, 'Fire!' He waited for the bullets.

The cry grew hoarse behind him. 'Fire! Fire!' A bell clanged. Brough reached the line of trees and heaved air into his ravaged lungs.

The duty officer, ringing the bell, heard anxious hands fumbling door handles along the corridor, and realised the patients were locked in. Six years ago he had been a sergeant in the Expeditionary Force, and a good one too; he was blowed if he would panic now. He went along the corridors, opening the doors one by one, sending the patients as he freed them along to the fire escape at the end of the building. Many were hysterical; many thought themselves lost in the war. Somehow, with calm and skill, he ushered them all out from the top corridor and descended to the lower one.

Already there were people in the corridor. Two orderlies always slept in the house, in case of trouble in the night, and the sergeant gave clear instructions. 'The fire's in the room at the end, Leonard's old room. For Christ's sake don't open that door: the fire'd spread and I saw someone jump from that window. But hurry and get the others out.'

Smoke was beginning to curl beneath David's door, blocking that exit, so they took the patients the other way, along the passage and through the house. The sergeant was surprised to see David Goodchild, hastily dressed in trousers and shirt and with his braces dangling from his waist, coming down the stairs with Mrs Penn, but there was no time to ask questions. At least that meant everybody was accounted for. 'Come *on*! Hurry up out!' he cried.

Sergeant Horton was the last to leave. The telephone was in the hall. He got through to the exchange in Buxley, along the valley, for the Grindlow exchange did not open till six, and told the telephonist of the fire. She thought he had been drinking, and told him so, but eventually she was convinced.

The patients waited outside. There was not much they could do. The sergeant counted them and then herded them together. Mary and David were grateful to be kept apart, and embarrassed by each other's presence.

The fire had scorched up the wall from the window of David's room, and from time to time they heard the ominous sounds from within that suggested the fire might be spreading, but so far as they could see it remained contained. The sergeant would not allow anyone within fifty feet of the burning building, so it was hard to be sure exactly what was happening; they found it curiously boring watching the fire, which took place within the walls, and started drifting apart on the lawns. The orderlies had to work hard simply to keep them together, and so the cause of the fire was not much discussed, although David was naturally thought to be involved. Someone who had seen him coming down the stairs held that he had been going to murder Mrs Penn after having first set fire to the building; the sergeant held his peace.

Jack Brough waited by the trees until his breath was bearable, and then struggled over the wire. A barb caught his flesh as he went over, and he found himself bleeding from a deep scratch in the thigh. His hands were scorched and painful. He shook his head, both to clear it and from despair.

He let himself scramble down the slope. The dawn was finding colours in the valley. He ran and scrambled on to the line.

Which way? he wondered. He started to go towards the station at Grindlow, and then remembered the signal-box and turned towards Wandlow and Buxley, only to stop again as he realised there was nothing for him there. Ragged and indecisive, he turned and turned again on the tracks like some bitter parody of a movie tramp, while the coming dawn gave him colour. 'I need a drink,' he decided, but he could do nothing about it.

The need, once recognised, flooded him and nauseated him. His hands and knees began to shake. 'Oh God, I need a drink.'

He started to go towards Grindlow again, unthinking. He walked past the signal-box and the paraffin shed. The lock-up was set back from the track, in case of sparks from passing locomotives, and Brough detoured towards it. He sat down against the shed with his head forward. His nausea was a tightening thread that drew his gut and forehead together and cramped his shoulders. Something bulged in the back of his throat and rubbed against his palate, but he could not force it up. The sun had climbed the hill ahead of him now, and poked a bloodshot eye at him. He stood again, unsteadily, and stumbled back to the track.

He reached the station. One of the morning staff was there. Brough shambled gauntly along the track. His face was black and his clothes were ruined. Ragged rents exposed burnt flesh. The eyes were wild and ringed with white. The railwayman hardly knew who it was.

Brough did not stop. The railwayman called after him, worriedly, and then called again. Brough continued forward, towards the slack and stupid mouth of the tunnel. Darkness gaped and gawped. The railwayman watched in disbelief as Brough walked into the tunnel, and then smelt the paraffin and was instantly suspicious.

Brough entered the damp and lady depths of the tunnel. The moisture on the walls showed as stars near the mouth, and the line was discernible in the gloom. Brough carried on to darkness.

His mind knew, but his body ceased to care. First there

was a humming in the lines, growing too fast for thought into a roar of distant light. The firebox glowed, the pistons sparked. There was a squeal that came too late, and then there was the impact. His body broke.

The milk train came to a halt. The firemen wanted to take a lamp and have a look, but the driver restrained him.

'You'll not find owt at moment. Chances are it's under us, whatever it were.'

'I'm sure I saw a man.'

'That's as may be. We're late.'

The fireman leaned from the footplate and waved the lamp. The feeble light found something white on the filthy aggregate. It was Jack Brough's hand, severed and palm down.

'Oh, Christ.'

'You'll not swear on my loco.'

'Look.'

The driver looked. He was unimpressed. 'Poor soul. Best think of him in our prayers.'

Queasiness made the fireman aggressive. 'Aren't we looking for the rest of him, then?'

'Not our job, is it?' said the driver. 'Come on. Can't do owt save report him anyhow, can we?'

'Aye,' said the fireman, reluctantly. 'Happen so.'

The driver eased the brake free and opened up the throttle. They were only a few hundred yards from the tunnel mouth, and beyond that they could see Grindlow Halt. The train pulled in slowly. There was a railwayman on the platform, waving furiously. Too late, thought the footplatemen: we've hit him. A stray spark rose past the stack, drifted north, and through to the office. There was a silly hiss that could be heard above the deeper sounds of the train, and then a roar. A slap of flame broke through the open doorway. They watched in wonder as the wooden buildings burnt. The railwayman on the platform was almost crying in frustration. He ran to the fire bucket. There was a sign by the hook:

These Buckets must be kept full of Clean Water, and used only in case of Fire.

In severe Frost they must be emptied and arranged close to a Water Tap, unless they can be temporarily kept in a Convenient Place where the Water will not freeze.

Derby. Jan. 1909. By Order.

The fire buckets were missing.

'It's not our day,' said the driver. He laughed a lot at this. And once he had begun he could not stop.

CHAPTER NINE

Because the firemen were divided between the station and Winfell, it was not until the rain began, at noon, that the Winfell fire was finally doused. In view of this, the damage was remarkably slight. David's room was gutted of course, as was the room above, but the flames had not spread sideways. The firemen praised the flat roof. 'Gets into the timbers as a rule, and then that's that, it spreads like wildfire, as the saying goes. But with these modern flat roofs, like, there's nowt much for fire to get a hold on, and no space to let flames breathe. It'd be that has saved the rest.' That, and the sergeant's sense.

A police inspector from Chesterfield was investigating the fire. As soon as the firemen, with bureaucratic reluctance, decided that the house was safe, the inspector set up his headquarters in the doctor's surgery. They interviewed the sergeant first.

'You're sure of this?' demanded the inspector.

The sergeant was suitably annoyed. 'If I said I saw a man running across lawn, then I saw a man running across lawn.'

'All right. But who was it? Can you give us a description?'

'Not really. I only looked at him for a moment, and then realised the place was on fire.'

'Man or woman?'

'Man.'

'Certain?' The sergeant nodded. 'How was he dressed?'

'Dark clothes, looked as if his jacket was on fire the way he was hitting at it.'

'Hat?'

'Can't remember seeing one.'

A second policeman was taking all this down. 'But presumably this man was Goodchild?'

'I'd say yes for certain, if I hadn't seen Goodchild coming downstairs of house after.'

'Could he have run round the house, gone upstairs, and been coming down again in the time between you seeing a man on the lawn and seeing Goodchild?'

'Aye. I reckon so.'

'What about his clothes? How was he dressed when he was coming down the stairs?'

'Like he was just putting them on.'

The inspector nodded intelligently. 'And he's a patient, this bloke Goodchild. What's he like? Unstable?'

'Fairly quiet. Always seems normal enough, but that don't mean much mind; there's several of them wouldn't say boo to a goose as a rule, but then they go funny and that's it.'

'And Goodchild's like that, you think?'

'Wouldn't be here if he was normal, would he?'

The inspector signalled that the second policeman should stop writing. 'Well,' he said. 'There doesn't seem to be much problem about what happened here, any road. I wonder how they're getting on at the station?'

The inspector asked to see David, who was not much help.

'I'd rather not say,' he told them.

'It'd go better for you if you did.'

'I'm afraid I can't.'

The inspector gave up. 'Look after him,' he told the policeman. 'We don't want him starting no more little blazes now, do we?' He could hear the telephone ringing in the hall. 'Answer that, will you. It'll be the doctor, most like; he'll have got the telegram by now.'

The police constable went down the stairs and answered the telephone; the inspector sat at the doctor's desk and played with the steel paper-knife. He heard the heavy footsteps of the constable returning.

'It's for you, sir. It's them at the station.'

'Right. I'll be down.' The inspector went confidently down the stairs. He spoke into the mouthpiece. 'Is that you, Stan? How are things? We've just about got this one licked I'd say.' And then he listened to what his colleague had to say, and his expression altered. 'I see,' he said from time to time. 'Right.'

He hung up the earpiece with a groan. 'Start again,' he told his constables. 'We'd best have another look at what's left in the burnt-out rooms. I'll not say what we're looking for, neither; let's just see what we can find. We've tried running before we could walk already this investigation.'

The doctor arrived with the rooks. Their sardonic harsh laughter greeted him as he was driven up the drive. Mary came out to meet him, and introduced him to the inspector.

They went together to see the damage. It was not as bad as the doctor had feared – particularly after he had seen the ruin of the station buildings, caused, so he was told, by a mere spark from a passing train – but none the less the blackening graffiti of the smoke-curls along the corridors and the sudden, skylit dereliction behind David's door succeeded in shocking him.

'How?' was all he could say for a moment, and then 'Why?' 'Seems he broke in through the window, poured paraffin on the bed, ignited it and left the same way.'

'So it was nothing to do with our patients.'

'No sir.'

'Well, thank goodness for that, at any rate. You've arrested the culprit.'

'I wouldn't exactly say that, sir. He's dead.' Briefly the inspector outlined the evidence against Brough: the cans of paraffin missing from the railway store; the empty cans which had been found in the two burnt-out buildings; the eyewitness accounts of Brough's appearance given by the sergeant, the signalman and the man on the station; two policemen's account of Brough's state that night.

'But why did he come here?' asked Penn.

'I suppose we'll never know that. He'd just lost his job, and that's why he burnt down the station we think, but as to him coming here, who's to say? I wondered if you might have some ideas, you being as it were a bit of an expert.'

'Not on the criminally insane,' Penn answered with a slight smile.

They left the devastated room. The crazy beams that had been left after the ceiling burnt through were rook black and rocking. They still supported the abandoned bedstead of the room upstairs. A chamberpot had miraculously survived the fire and lay, open-mouthed, against the charred remains of a wardrobe. The rain and the firemen's hose had made a morass of the ashes. Penn was glad to get out.

'You're sure about all this?' he asked.

'What makes you ask?'

'Well, what about David Goodchild? He'd have been locked into the room. What happened about him?'

Mary was walking ahead of the other two. She did not dare stop or turn round.

'Nothing to concern us,' replied the inspector, airily. 'Beyond the scope of our investigation, as the saying goes.'

'How odd. Have you asked him?'

'Oh, yes, sir. We've asked him.' The doctor waited to hear more; the inspector, however, was silent.

'Well?' asked the doctor, as they reached the end of the passage and walked into the scullery.

'Like I say, sir, it's beyond the scope of our investigations. But there's plenty of others might tell you, I'm sure.'

The inspector felt vaguely justified in the malice he felt towards David; he felt David had almost deliberately misled him. On the other hand, he was damned if he was going to explain to Dr Penn that one of his patients was sleeping with his wife. Penn, intrigued and diverted by the mystery, led the way up the stairs to Mary's sitting-room.

'You'll have a cup of tea, inspector, before you go?'

They sat facing one another across the sitting-room. The inspector had left. The patients had been, where necessary, moved to the attic rooms of the house. It was growing dark. The doctor bent to pick the newspaper from beside his chair. 'God! Yesterday's.'

'Clive,' began Mary.

'Yes?'

She looked away from him. 'How did your lecture go?' He must work it out soon, she thought desperately, and yet she could not tell him herself. This way there was always the chance it might blow over.

'Oh, that.' He had genuinely almost forgotten it. 'Very well, I think. Your father came. He told me he enjoyed it.'

'Good,' said Mary. 'Good.'

Conversation stopped. The doctor stretched and then smiled, remembering.

'That telegram of yours really scared me, you know. "FIRE AT WINFELL STOP COME BACK AT ONCE STOP MARY." I imagined the whole place had been burnt to the ground.' His voice suddenly stopped. He felt something vast and dreadful yawn open inside him. 'My God!' he said, aghast.

'What is it?' she asked, though she knew.

'David was with you.' She neither spoke nor looked at him. His mind swung vertiginously over the chasm. 'I'll find somewhere else to sleep,' he said, hoping to hurt her, praying that he still could.

'Don't be silly,' she found herself saying. 'All the rooms are full now we've had to move the patients.'

He had to say it, had to believe he could cause her pain. 'I'll have David Goodchild's room then, and he can sleep with you.'

She was shocked into a new silence, and then ugly, untheatrical tears rimmed her eyes and smeared her powder. He stared at her, concentrating on his anger so that he need not think of other things.

'Is that what you think?' she asked him at last.

He was shamed but militant. 'Yes!'

'It wasn't like that.'

He breathed scornfully through his nose, still concentrating on holding that hard firm reliable anger in the face of his grief.

'We were talking. About poetry. Clive, believe me.' She found a weapon, unexpectedly, and then used it. 'If you think that, then you're sick, Clive. I can't live with you if you believe that.'

He closed his eyes. His face was drawn. In a voice that was soft and not quite familiar to him, he said, 'Let's go to bed.'

They made love that evening, and she was beautiful again, but afterwards she slept and he found he could not rest. She lay against his shoulder heavily while his mind conjured spiteful words. Adultery; cuckold. He eased himself from under her possessive weight and rolled away. The harsh, archaic terms tumbled in his head. They were judgments. Thou shall not commit adultery. A cuckold and his horns. His mind made cruel, ironic puns. Cuckold; cuckoo. A cuckoo in the nest. Cuckolded by a cuckoo. In the cuckoo's nest. He did not sleep all night.

'I've been feeling rather guilty about you, David,' said the doctor. 'After all, we haven't had a chat since the fire, and that's nearly two weeks ago. I haven't forgotten you though: in fact I've been checking one or two things. It's time we had a good long chat.'

The doctor said it again. It still sounded threatening. Drop that bit about checking things, he decided: it's that which sounds so sinister.

He searched David out, and found him in the garden. Afterwards he looked for George. He had some good news for George.

'Come in, David. Sit right down. Now, you've told me a lot about your past, your home and school and so on. But what we haven't talked about yet so much is the war. I expect you'll agree that the war has been crucial in the way things have turned out for you, and I expect also that the war will involve many painful memories. So rather than causing you pain – we wouldn't want to do that, of course, would we – let's talk about your poetry.'

David reached for his cigarettes. The doctor sat above him on a dining-chair, while he reclined in an armchair.

'Let me,' said the doctor, offering a light.

'Thank you.'

'Good. Now, let's begin by looking at a poem or two. This one, for instance: "Charles Curragh". A very fine poem indeed, to my mind.

Last night I dreamt of Charles Curragh, who drowned
In his own blood, was slashed across the throat
While we looked on or, gauchely, looked around.
He was our first casualty. I wrote
A line or two about his death; I quote:
'Although my friend is dead, this much I saw:
Red blood has stained to English red his coat,
The noble red our English troops once wore,
And Charlie Curragh's joined those gone before.'

I was very young.

'A beautiful poem,' continued the doctor. 'And what is of course particularly admirable is its truthfulness. The way you acknowledge the naïvity of the first poem and comment on it. And of course the extremely clever way you build it into the new poem. Based on a dream, too, which has particular interest for me as you can imagine. It is all true, of course?'

David did not look at the doctor, but pulled on his cigarette. 'I don't quite know what you mean.'

'It all happened in the way you describe, of course?'

'Well . . . I suppose so.'

'"Well . . . I suppose so?" What sort of answer is that? We'll try a more straightforward question then: is it true?'

'Yes.' David was emphatic in his quiet way.

'Are you sure? Is it really all the literal truth?'

'Not literally, perhaps,' decided David. 'But it is true.'

'Are we certain about this? Can it be true, but not literally true? I wouldn't have thought so. But we'll leave that. What parts aren't true?'

David did not answer. The doctor passed the manuscript poem over. 'Perhaps you'd better read it yourself. I mean, there was an earlier poem about Charles Curragh, for instance? The piece in quotation marks was genuinely from an earlier poem?'

'Well. Not exactly. I might have changed it a bit, here or there.'

'Changed it a bit? But surely the whole point is that you are commenting on how your way of seeing an incident changed. If the earlier poem wasn't genuine, how are we to believe the rest of it? There was an earlier poem about Charles Curragh, I hope?'

'Well, actually, no.'

'No! You'll be telling me next that there wasn't even anybody called Charles Curragh!'

David swallowed. 'There wasn't. It's just a name, one I thought up.'

The doctor nodded. 'I know. I checked. The whole poem,' he said quietly, 'is a tissue of lies.'

'No,' said David, weakly. 'It's a poem.'

'Does that excuse the lies? Its whole effect comes from its apparent truthfulness. Without that, it's nothing.'

'No,' he repeated. 'It's just a poem.'

'*Just a poem?* That's a strange thing for a poet to say. I thought a poem was some sort of personal statement? I thought that poets saw things more truly and accurately than the rest of us? I thought that was what made them special? That's what my wife says anyway. And you'll have talked about that together, in your long intimate conversations, I'm sure.'

'I don't know,' admitted David, comprehensively.

'It seems very strange to me. I mean, there really does seem to be some confusion here. About what is true and what isn't. But then,' said the doctor, relenting, dropping his voice to the practised, unctuous tones of concern, 'that's why you are here, isn't it?'

'I don't know what you mean.'

'You're here, David, because you can't tell what is true from what is untrue, what is real from what is not. That's the case isn't it?'

'I suppose so.'

'Aren't you sure?'

'I don't know.'

'Your life has been a lie, David,' said the doctor with a voice rich with concern. 'What we must do is trace the beginning of that lie. We must sort out when the lie began, and then perhaps we will be able to do something for you.'

David nodded. He suspected, strongly, that Penn knew about him and Mary, for what else would account for his aggressive attitude? He decided to let Penn have his say.

'Dr Freud would say, for instance, that it all stemmed from some childhood incident. That incident at school perhaps, when the older boy touched your hair, could have been the beginning of the lie. Do we know for certain that's all he touched?'

David nodded again.

'Are we certain though, David? I mean, what if he'd touched you somewhere else? What if this big handsome prefect had touched you somewhere private? What if he'd given you an erection? He did make you have an erection, didn't he David? Did he lie you on his bed? Did he take off your clothes? Did he penetrate you David? Did he do that?'

'No!' said David, shaken into vehemence. 'It wasn't like that at all!'

'Did he corrupt you, David? I expect he did. I expect that's why you have this interest in married women. Because you don't like being a homosexual, do you David? It's dirty, isn't it David? And it's wrong. It's against the law. But you can put it into a married woman, David, and it's almost the same as having a man. Two birds with one stone. David Goodchild, the seducer, seducing women with his poems, and all the time it is David Goodchild the homosexual who is looking for the satisfaction from the sex. That's it, isn't it?'

David mumbled his denial.

'It must have been difficult for you in the army. Did they find out? Did the men you were leading find out? Or was it something else that made them hold you in such contempt?'

David looked up. There was a genuine fear in his eyes. I hate this man, the doctor reminded himself.

'Oh yes. I found out about Charles Curragh; I found out one or two other things as well. You couldn't do it, could you. You couldn't lead them. That's why you let them die. 15 June 1918, wasn't it? Your first breakdown, according to the records.'

David was white now. His teeth dug into his lower lips. The doctor continued, remorselessly.

'How many was it? Twenty? Twenty-five? More? It

was a massacre, David. And it was all your fault, wasn't it?'

'I forgot,' David managed to say.

'Forgot! No, it wasn't as simple as that. They held you in contempt, you wanted your revenge. You didn't forget. You chose not to tell them. Think back, David. Think back. After all, you've been living a lie about your sexuality for years. We've seen how good you are at believing your own lies. Look at that poem. Mary was convinced, wasn't she? She believed in the poems and in you. You convinced her; I'll bet you've convinced yourself. I'll bet you believe you forgot. But we know better now, don't we? You think back. You think back to 15 June 1918. It isn't surprising you took refuge in a sort of madness afterwards. No one could live with that sort of guilt. But if we're going to cure you David we're going to have to sort this one out. So think back. Think back to 15 June 1918. Think back!'

'We'll be expecting a big push any time now, I fear,' says the colonel. 'There's no secret. Since the Russians gave in the Hun has been building up dreadfully. I say, Goodchild, don't hog the port.'

I pass it on quickly. Another push. My dinner is pain in my gut. I know this feeling. It is dread.

I swallow down the port. Its warmth gives me no comfort. 'Drank that in a bit of a hurry didn't you, old man,' says the padre. 'Blood of Christ, don't-you-know.'

I gag. 'Excuse me,' I mutter. 'Need some air.' Others mutter too. In this Mess no one gets up before the colonel. I do not care. Blood of Christ! What sort of religion is this? Water into wine? Wine into blood? It frightens me.

I get beyond the door and shut it with my back. The dread floods into my bowels. I sweat at my face and back.

'You all right, old man?' It is the padre. The colonel probably sent him; he hasn't the guts to do anything off his own bat.

Who am I to talk of guts? Mine are loose with dread. 'No,' I reply.

'Bit of a funk, what? Can I get you anything?'

'No.' And then, 'Yes, some water.' Get rid of him. He goes back to the Mess; I go outside.

It was once a half-decent château. I walk down the steps. There are soldiers cleaning the cars outside. They should salute me, and don't. I ought to insist, but can't. I hear something muttered behind my back, and ignore it. Why should I care what they think?

There is no privacy in a war, and I want to be alone, but there's nowhere left to go, so I return.

'Feeling better, old man?' asks the padre.

'Fine,' I lie.

'Night duty tonight?' He thinks he is being subtle, drawing my attention to it in case I haven't noticed.

'Yes,' I reply. I loathe his company, yet it is the only company I get. I loathe being categorised as some sort of failure: and why should I be. Why should I try to be a good soldier? I'm a poet, for Heaven's sake. A poet.

'I wonder how much the colonel knows?' the padre is asking. 'About the German push I mean. It's not like him to tell us anything unless it is really important.'

I agree.

'I hope the casualties are low,' he continues. 'Funerals are beastly.'

'Good God.' He looks at me, awaiting my inevitable apology for blaspheming before a man of the cloth. I turn on my heel and walk off in silence.

It is a mile or so to the trenches, and a mile or so beyond that to the front lines. I've only an hour, so if I am to walk it I must be quick. I decide to walk, despite the weight of my dread. I need to clear my mind.

I pass rows and rows of bivouacs. The men are lighting their fires to keep the crepuscular creepy-crawlies away. I have no fire, only my cigarette, and am followed by a grey city of midges that traffics around my head.

The road is muddy, barely a track, and has been broken in places by bombs. Duckboards lie across the deeper pot-holes. The shell-holes have to be skirted.

I reach the supply trenches. First-aid men, ambulance drivers and stretcher bearers relax and drink tea from enamel mugs. The duckboards here are ancient rotting hulks that are slimy with trodden clay and do nothing to help us stand. I tramp over them carefully, passing games of cards and men writing letters. The route zig-zags back and forth. Sometimes an abandoned parapet indicates an old front line, or a trench wall is stained yellow by lyddite. It has been a long, long war. No one remembers who dug out these trenches; no one even remembers which side.

A strange, moist, subterranean world. I have never seen an open sewer – I have read that the river Fleet was an open sewer, which seems appropriate – but I imagine it would be much like this. Only quieter.

But we are not allowed to complain. This is a quiet sector, a cushy trench. We are told so every day. 'Think about the other fellow,' says the colonel. 'We've got it easy here, lowest casualties in the brigade.'

A quiet sector. Until the next big push.

The doctor had stood up and walked to the window. He looked outside at the cynical rooks. He did not need to listen to David's stumbling memories. He did not even want to any more. He had his revenge and it was not sweet. If he let himself, the doctor could feel sorry, but he did not let himself. He clung still to that solid, certain, dependable anger, for without it he would be quite empty. He watched a black rook pivot on the point of a wing and turn, effortlessly, in mid-flight. The arch, swift elegance of the bird! Behind him, he heard David shamble through his tale. The words were indistinct; the memory was clearer than all life.

My platoon waits in a lateral trench, drinking steaming tea. It was not so bad before the sergeant died, but now it is impossible. They ignore my every word. They despise me. They call me Lillah, after the actress Lillah McCarthy. I cannot remember why.

I have instructions to give them. 'Get the men quiet please corporal,' I say, knowing he will make no effort.

'Shut up, you lot,' says the corporal. He does not even stand. He is playing draughts.

'Put that away,' I tell him. He ignores me. 'I said put it away.'

'What, this?' he says, indicating his gun which lies against the trench side. His opponent laughs.

'The draughtboard,' I say. They are getting me angry. They always get me angry.

'Wait till the end of the game,' he says. 'Sir.'

'Put it away now!;

'Lillah's getting waxy!' chants a voice from along the trench. I do not know whose voice it is. I'm not sure I want to know.

'Be quiet!' I yell. They are, or almost so, and I hear the click of draughts on the board. I spin round, furious.

'Just putting it away,' says the corporal, with infuriating calmness. 'No need to get excited.'

'Just get them to listen to me,' I tell him.

'Hey lads,' he says, standing and facing them now. 'Shut up and listen, eh?' They laugh and talk amongst themselves. 'They don't want to,' he tells me.

I push along the trench, blind with impotence. 'Be quiet. Be quiet. Be quiet.' I have orders to read out. 'Be quiet. Listen to the orders.'

Again I achieve a semblance of hush. 'B Company Platoons to occupy forward sector trenches 16N to 7SE . . .'

'Trafalgar Square,' says a soldier, using their slang, and the others laugh.

'Platoons to line by numbers at 18.54 precisely for recce. duty in forward sector.'

They are all talking now. They have heard it all before. Am I the only officer in France who has this problem? I can't believe I am, yet you rarely hear of others. I stop and start again, and get wolf-whistled from the few who are listening to my words at all. Then the jeering begins. I am a poet. This does not matter to me. This is the war, it is not reality. I will escape from here. The war will end. I am a poet. These men are nothing to do with me.

'Sir?' It is the corporal speaking. I turn on him. He smiles peacefully at me. '18.54 we should get there?'

'That's right.' I have read my way through the orders. I fold them up and put them in my top pocket in the usual manner.

'It's 18.54 now sir.'

'Get a move on then!' I prod some life into a soldier. He grins at me. 'Come on. We're late.'

It becomes a chant. 'We're late; we're late.'

'Line up along the trench!' I shout. And they do, after a fashion. 'Lead them off, corporal,' I shout from the back.

The chant changes. 'We're off; we're off.'

We twist left and then right, the corporal leading. We go through the trench they call Carshalton Road and turn into Pound Street. I follow, inadequately waving my pistol. A machine-gun starts ahead, and when the machine-gun stops the screaming begins. Ahead of me, massacred, is my platoon. I stand at the corner that leads into Pound Street.

'56W Lateral is not to be used because of enfilade.' I read those words and no one heard. Not even me. I hear the men in the trench calling out, but cannot even move towards them because the machine-gun would open up again. My mind is crisper and clearer now than for a long time. There is no choice. I must go mad. I rock back and forth on my heels. I breathe sharp shallow breaths through nose and through mouth. I drop my pistol and run my hands through my hair, over my face, around the back of my neck. My tin helmet dangles before me like a nosebag.

My eyes are wide, gasping with my breath. Something must burst. I step forward and into Pound Street. I step over the last of the corpses.

No bullets fly. I fight off this knowledge of reality. I do not want to know if I will live or die. That does not concern me. I step over a body. I am laughing. I move further forward and laugh some more. In my neck there is a vicious pain, but there is a new lightness about my shoulders that I have not known before. It is as though the tension has fled from me. I find my corporal. He has been roughly torn in half. I cradle his upper parts in my arms and rock him gently. Lullaby, lullaby. You should have listened, I tell him, and he laughs and agrees. You never learn until it is too late, I say. His hair is full of blood and so is mine. It spikes and matts to branches. In the woods by my old home there are wych-elms. They have faces in their bark. The wounded scream and bark. They have never shut up when I have told them. Their voices pull my flesh and make it raw. It tears from me in gobbets. Their teeth are out. I had not known before that they were hounds.

I am Actaeon, ripped open by my hounds. Their slavering mouths run with my juices. My innards hang in loops and dangling tassels. If I saw Diana naked I cannot recall when. It is the only thing I cannot recall. The rest tattoos my brain and cannot be removed.

CHAPTER TEN

Mary touched the edge of her husband's hand where it rested on the back of the pew. Without taking his eyes from the procession, he raised his little finger and let her hand slip under his, pressing it tight against the wood. George went by in black and white: the surplice was freshly laundered. He sang as he walked, in his fine pure voice, and his face, despite the scars of innumerable shaving accidents and the blackheads about his nose, was dignified into a kind of beauty. He took his place in the choir-stalls. Mary saw his anxious eyes search them out among the patch-patterned congregation, and then his eyes met hers and he smiled. He was radiant; he was serene; and Mary wanted to cry.

After the service they waited for George, talking with Morrison as they did so.

'It was all a ploy to get your husband to church,' said the vicar, smiling at them both. 'I knew that he wouldn't be able to resist coming himself to see George in the choir. Now we have to make sure he comes back every week.'

'George will be allowed back then, you think?' asked Mary.

'Oh, yes. The choir have quite taken to him, like a mascot. They'll be wanting to take him to their cricket matches soon. And he does have a superb voice.'

They felt proud, like parents receiving a good school report. George, accompanied by a jovial baritone, came out of the vestry door and walked round the church to the porch where the Penns stood.

'Did you enjoy that?' asked Mary.

'You don't need ask,' said the baritone. 'Look at face on him.' George grinned beatifically. 'Are you in an 'urry to get him back, or is there time for a swift drink? Rest of choir'll be in the Sir William. It'd do him good.'

Mary looked at her husband encouragingly. 'All right,' he said. 'What harm could there be? Nothing alcoholic for George though, be absolutely certain of that.'

'You not be coming yoursen, then?'

'We'll wait outside. It's a lovely morning,' said Mary.

'Right you are then,' said the baritone. 'Come on Georgie-Porgie. Time for a swift one. We'll have a bit of a sing-song too, if tha likes.'

'I'd better be getting up to the vicarage,' said Morrison. 'I've a group of parishioners to see. Well, it's been charming having you here. You will be back next week? And you will bring George? That's all right then. Goodbye.'

'Goodbye,' they called.

They walked across the bridge and through the village. The Sir William was at the foot of the hill at the far side of the valley. Well before they reached it the sound of dogs yapping told them there was a meet.

'I didn't know they hunted on a Sunday,' said the doctor.

'Any day,' said Mary. 'Though this won't be the fox hunt. It's the hare-coursers: they meet at the Sir William.' She found herself talking too much and could not stop. 'At this time of year Sunday is the only day they can hunt, because they're busy with the harvest.'

They did not talk very often any more, but today had been a good day. With renewed confidence she took his hand again. You have to forget things, thought Mary. She willed him to read her mind.

There was a confusion of shouts up the hill, and the

hare-coursing began. The street was flooded with hounds; their droopy mouths dripped slack strands of drool. The doctor moved Mary from the stream, and sheltered her as the dogs went by. An impetuous kiss brushed her forehead. She looked up at him gratefully.

The hounds made their way to the wheat fields on the southern side of the valley. A reaping machine was tugged by a horse. It made generous, unwieldy bales that the farm boys lugged to the lane for collection. They looked up from their work at the sound of the chase. The hounds were snuffling through the neighbouring fields, doubling on a trail and doubling back. There was a sudden yell. A hare fled from the stalks ahead of the horse. The hounds were quick on its tail, scampering through the harvest and spilling the grains. The men threshed through the waist-deep field behind them.

'Oi!' shouted the farmer. 'Clear off. Keep 'em out,' he yelled to his boys, but they had dropped their bales and joined with the chase.

The hare was cornered in the next field. It ran at the drystone walls again and again but could not make its escape, and so dashed into the advancing pack. By the time the huntsmen came it was a handful of skin and bone.

Mary and her husband watched from the wall of the Sir William, sitting beneath the gallows-hanging sign. They saw the fervour of the hunt and the coup, and were glad to have missed the aftermath.

'I'll get George,' said the doctor.

The hunt moved off in search of new prey.

George was sitting in the middle of a large group. Appropriately, perhaps encouraged by the hunt, he sang a song he had sung once in a school play.

> An old hare hoar,
> And an old hare hoar,
> Is very good meat in Lent;
> But a hare that is hoar

> Is too much for a score,
> When it hoars ere it be spent.

'Come on, Mercutio,' said the doctor.

'You knew it?' asked George, overwhelmed.

'Come on. Not so excited, eh fellow? It's time to go home. Say goodbye.'

'Goodbye,' he said obediently.

They walked back to their motor-car.

'Everyone aboard,' called the doctor driving off. The car was new and Penn steered it carefully around the narrow lanes. Another car came up behind them. It could not get past them and so was forced to follow.

'What a big car,' said Mary.

'It's a Twenty-Five Horsepower Vauxhall. I saw a lot of them in the war. They were used as staff cars.'

'Isn't that Mrs Goodchild in the back? I didn't know she'd got a car.'

'Is it?' asked the doctor. 'She probably hired it in Sheffield.' He made himself laugh, though his good humour had suddenly gone. 'There isn't the demand for staff cars, these days.' He thought of Mary next to him, and thought of her thinking of David. It was almost too much to bear.

They turned through the gates and up the drive. The powerful Vauxhall parked next to their 4-seater Bean. They exchanged formal greetings on the turning space in front of the house. They were very kind to her.

'Shall we fetch David?' asked Mary.

'Where is he now?' Mrs Goodchild wondered. 'Don't disturb him if he's busy.'

The doctor exchanged a concerned glance with his wife. She doesn't realise, he thought. 'He'll be in the garden,' said Mary.

'We'll leave him for a little while, shall we?' said Mrs Goodchild.

'I'm so glad you could come,' said the doctor, stiffly.

Meeting Mrs Goodchild had unnerved him unexpectedly. 'But, as I said in my letter, I really think it would be better for David if he left Winfell.' He suddenly realised what he had done: 'I must see about getting his things loaded into your motor car,' he said, backing away. 'So useful you could bring a motor.' He had broken this woman's son. 'So much more private than the railroad.' He had broken his patient. He left them.

'Shall we go in?' asked Mary.

Mrs Goodchild followed. 'He was happy here, until the fire?'

'Oh, yes. Very,' said Mary. 'Until the fire.'

'Your husband explained in his letter. Everything was destroyed, I believe.'

'Everything he kept in the room. There are some things, things the patients don't often need and so on, we keep in store. Clive – Dr Penn – is sorting them out at the moment.'

'Were a lot of his poems destroyed?'

'I'm afraid so. We had copies of some.'

'Has he written any recently? Since the fire?'

'No.'

'But he will write again?'

Mary paused. 'I don't know,' she admitted. 'There's a poem here I'd like you to see,' she said quickly. 'It was the last one he wrote, before the fire.'

Mrs Goodchild took the manuscript from Mary, and took her glasses from her bag.

> The meadow dawns to day, and pastel dew
> Is pathed by darker tracks: the March hare here
> Courted and cavorted. Mad Carew
> Was fortified by love, and thus could dare
> Steal the idol's eye; likewise, the hare
> Has danced here for his doe at break of day.
>
> I know well this mad hare: he shares my moon
> And dances in the month whence I was born.

I know his soul: he's heard the same March tune
Fanfare in the hush and meadow, moan
The mournful wood. It marches in the bone
Of the dancing hare. It marches mine.

It marched me to the hunt, the hidden booth
At the meadow's edge. I loaded death
Into my gun and aimed. I felt, in truth,
The mad March hare was brother of my birth
And wanted to hold fire, but jealous earth
Outweighed our moon. I fired, and shot us both.

The same tune marched to war. At the front line
I've sometimes felt the same about the Hun
Haring towards me in some mad design
Of another's making, till the forlorn
Sound of firing, a strained, staccato horn,
Wails across the wire and he is slain.

Yet, Hun or hare, a corpse is just a sack.
It might be made to move by the sick jerk
Of random bullets bludgeoning its back
But it contains no life. I watch it soak
Back to jealous earth, and chat, and joke.
The pity that I feel's for my own sake.

Mrs Goodchild stood in silence when she had finished.

'We saw a hare hunt today,' said Mary, conversationally.

'I'm sure,' Mrs Goodchild replied, distantly. 'You never really got to know David, did you?' she said.

'I don't know what you mean.'

'Nor what David means,' she said, relishing the play on words. She was proud now and firm. 'What you seem to have neglected is his genius.'

Mary turned away. 'I think we should go out and see him now,' she said.

The doctor stood at his surgery window. He lit a cigarette, drew on it, pinched it out. I can't go back, he realised. I can't face them. He looked outside. His service revolver was in his filing cabinet. The rooks were gone from the trees. He closed his eyes.

The two women went out to the garden. 'I think I'd better warn you about David,' said Mary.

'Warn me?' said Mrs Goodchild. Her voice had a new edge.

'I think my husband told you in his letter that David had had a collapse. It's just that he – he isn't any better.'

'How is he? Is he worse?'

'I'm afraid he is.'

They stood at the back of the annexe, looking down on the neat garden and the new-mown lawn. A furry burr of bee buzzed the roses, ricocheting helplessly. David sat in a canvas chair. Despite the clear day there was a blanket over his knees.

His eyes were open. He saw the blue sky and the breeze trill in the leaves. He saw the bee turn topsy-turvy in the flowers, and right itself, and drink. There was a moon to be seen through the daylight, and he watched this moon-in-exile's pallid shape.

His mouth was open too. His tongue swung loose and impotent. A dribble of saliva messed his chin. The women walked together towards him, but stopped when they heard the shot.

A NOTE ON THE AUTHOR

Richard Burns, born in 1958, is a graduate of Lancaster and Sheffield universities. He was selected for *The Gregory Anthology: The Best of Young British Poets* in 1984, and in 1987 he was Writer in Residence at Huddersfield Polytechnic. In the same year he won a Hawthornden Fellowship for poetry, and more recently was Visiting Professor of Creative Writing at New England College. He now lives in Sheffield with his wife and three children, and reviews regularly for the *Independent*.